It was on the tip of his tongue to tell Connor about his attraction to Kit.

Griffin could keep it in check. He wasn't a slave to his hormones. Too much was at stake for him to give in to his feelings. Instead, he made the point that mattered most. "My wife died because I couldn't protect her. What makes you think I can keep Kit safe?"

"This situation is nothing like what happened with Beth. What could you have done differently? No one blames you for Beth's death except you."

At the mention of his wife's name, disgust for himself and anger at her killer renewed. "I ask myself that every day."

"The answer eludes you because there is no answer. You couldn't have done anything. What happened with Beth was a terrible atrocity, but protecting Kit will be different. You will be at her side around the clock. She is your sole mission."

Griffin didn't care for his body's response to hearing that. As a red-blooded man, he wanted to be close to Kit. As an operative, he wasn't qualified to protect her.

* * *

If you're on Twitter, tell us what you think of Harlequin Romantic Suspense! #harlequinromsuspense

Dear Reader,

Kit Walker is great with technology. But people—not so much. When her past working on a top secret government project comes back to haunt her, Kit has to rely on Griffin Brooks, an operative for the West Company. Kit doesn't trust him. Her experiences with men have been rocky and Griffin is far too callous and demanding. Except he's also drop-dead gorgeous, and Kit finds that hard to ignore and makes it even harder to keep her distance from him.

Tough, competent and cool under fire, Griffin has been sent by the West Company to ensure Kit's safety. Griffin is unexpectedly drawn to the awkward and unassuming woman he has been assigned to protect. Griffin has something to prove to himself and won't let anything get in the way of his mission. When the operation goes sideways and Griffin and Kit are forced on the run, Griffin must decide to either protect Kit or his heart.

The characters in this book were inspired by the amazing computer scientists I've worked with. I hope my fellow geeks find and enjoy their happy endings!

Best,

C.J. Miller

www.CJ-Miller.com

DELTA FORCE DESIRE

C.J. Miller

H HARLEQUIN® ROMANTIC SUSPENSE

Recycling programs
for this product may
not exist in your area.

ISBN-13: 978-0-373-27992-0

Delta Force Desire

Copyright © 2016 by C.J. Miller

Printed in U.S.A.

C.J. Miller loves to hear from her readers and can be contacted through her website, cj-miller.com. She lives in Maryland with her husband and three children. C.J. believes in first loves, second chances and happily-ever-after.

Visit C.J.'s Author Profile page at Harlequin.com, or cj-miller.com, for more titles.

To Noelle, for the light, love and joy
you bring to our lives each day.

Chapter 1

Kaitlyn "Kit" Walker was not rocking the slinky, glittery red dress. On the hanger, it had looked great. On her, it was garish and borderline indecent. Kit had left her bedroom wearing it only because her sister Marissa had insisted she blend with her model friends. One problem with that: Kit wasn't a model. She didn't even photograph that well.

Kit felt awkward and uncomfortable. She was certain she looked like a sausage stuffed into a too-tiny casing, bulging in the wrong places. All she needed was for the seams or zipper to pop and make her humiliation complete. At least no one was looking at her. She was about seven inches too short and thirty pounds too heavy for anyone at the party to be staring at her when so much eye candy was prancing around her, giggling and taking selfies.

Kit preferred to fly under the radar of the constant clicking of cameras on smartphones. She wasn't anything to post about on social media, and she liked it that way. She preferred to remain out of the public eye.

Kit only had to stay at the swanky rooftop party until they sang happy birthday to her sister and cut the cake—the thousand-dollar, perfectly decorated cake Marissa and her friends wouldn't touch. Some celebrity baker had prepared it. Would he be insulted if no one bothered to eat it?

It was nearly dusk and the terrace was aglow with silver spherical lanterns. The serving bars were illuminated with fluorescent green. The whole party was not Kit's scene.

At least their brother seemed to be having a good time. He was flirting and talking with the beautiful women. Their mother was in her element. A former Miss California, sipping champagne, wearing a couture gown, and talking to Marissa's agent, her mother was all toothy smiles.

Kit's phone was tucked in her clutch. Her fingers stretched toward it. She had promised Marissa she would socialize and not type on her phone the entire time, but no one was speaking to her, and it was unlikely anyone would. She had nothing in common with actors and models and photographers. She was probably the only woman on the roof who wasn't regularly featured in the gossip columns. She couldn't be in the gossip columns; her life depended on it. If someone saw her picture and recognized her as anyone other than Kit Walker, she was screwed.

Kit swirled the lemon-lime cola in her wineglass. She would have drunk it straight from the can, but the bartender had given her such a look when she requested it, she decided she would use a glass.

A light breeze blew, and Kit shivered. Was being cold an excuse to leave? It was July in Southern California and no one else seemed uncomfortable, but Kit wasn't accustomed to being half-naked. Her legs were bare. Her arms were bare. Her shoulders were bare. How did people relax when they were dressed like this?

Goose bumps formed on her arms, and she turned, sensing someone watching her. She pasted on a smile in case it was her sister. Kit could pretend she was enjoying people-watching. Watching beautiful people seducing and flattering each other was an activity that didn't involve her phone. After the party was over, these beautiful people would go home with companions as attractive as they were.

Kit would go home alone, water her plants and go to bed. That was okay. She didn't want someone coming home with her.

She didn't see her sister, but a man was watching Kit drink her soda. A good-looking man. Was he trying to place her? Wondering why she was at this party? He had the smoldering, sexy look down pat. He must be a model or an actor. His hair was longer, reaching to the tops of his ears, and he was dressed in a black T-shirt, dark blue jeans and boots. Though his expression was serious, he almost seemed amused. Her defenses heightened. She wasn't in the mood to be teased. She'd heard every joke in the world about being the ugly sister to supermodel Marissa.

She was aware she wasn't as gorgeous as her sister. Since she had been a baby, she'd been compared to her sister, and Kit did not rank on any magazine's list as hot or tempting. At some point, looks wouldn't matter as much, and someone would recognize her genius. But in this space and at this time, looks mattered; brains didn't. Maybe when she and Marissa were in their sixties, someone would finally stop snapping pictures of Marissa long enough to realize that Kit was smart.

Kit didn't blame her sister. Marissa was a good person with a warm heart, but the media cared only how she looked, what she wore and where she partied. Kit and her sister were both underestimated.

The man started toward her. Kit slid off the stool. She checked that her dress was pulled down in the back and tried to flee. It was juvenile, but she didn't want to have an actual conversation with a handsome man or fend off a joke about her.

Kit didn't get far. With her ridiculous borrowed shoes, she had to walk like a clopping horse. The roof was too jam-packed, and unlike her sister, who strode through a room and parted the crowd, Kit had no such effect on the people around her.

The man reached her and smiled. The smile shifted his looks from handsome to drop-dead gorgeous. Her knees locked and her breasts tightened and she cursed her body's complete overreaction. Maybe this was how men felt when they looked at her sister. If so, she understood their obsession with Marissa a bit more. Standing in front of this man, it was hard to look away.

"You're Kit Walker, right?" he asked.

Kit blinked at him and then looked behind her. He'd said her name, but was he actually looking for her? She could think of only one reason why he would. "If you are trying to meet my sister through me, Marissa doesn't make a mockery of me by allowing men to use me to get to her." It had happened at least five times in the past. It was humiliating for Kit, having a man pretend to like her only to flat-out ignore her once he was in Marissa's presence. Marissa hated it. Kit wasn't a fan, either.

"I have no interest in your sister," the man said. His voice was deep and slightly gravelly. Like the voice of a man who was used to being in charge and in control. Maybe an actor, then. Or a director.

"You'd be the first and only man on the planet." She laughed so she didn't sound completely bitter, but it wasn't funny. It was true and painful. When she was younger, she used to imagine a man would come into their lives and see something in her that made her more attractive than Marissa.

"Is there a place we could speak in private?" he asked.

"I don't sneak off to closets with strangers," she said.

He frowned, and she mourned the loss of his amazing smile. His eyes were flat and serious. "I have no plans to put you in a closet. I do have something important to speak with you about. It's a sensitive matter. I am familiar with your work."

Her stomach dropped. His voice gave away he wasn't referring to her job at the florist. It had been four years since she had worked as a computer scientist, and she had put the past behind her. Though she sometimes woke in the night in a cold sweat, nightmares about her previous work hounding her, Kit had built a safe life for herself.

Kit held up her hands and backed away. "Stay away from me." How had anyone found her? She had been exceedingly careful.

She turned to flee and he grabbed her wrist, preventing her escape. The party went on around her as if no one was aware of what was happening to her. Being socially invisible might get her killed. "If you don't let me go, I will scream. My sister has a security team here. They will…tackle you." Kit had seen her sister's bodyguards grapple with or hit men who lunged at her sister either trying to cop a feel or take a picture up her dress. It was comical how easily her bodyguards kept pests away.

But this man was more than a pervert with a mission. This man was a threat. He wouldn't be flicked to the side.

He released her. "Shade sent me."

The words came on a whisper, carrying a heavy message. Shade, a name from her past, ancient history. Shade was known for being ridiculously principled and scrupulously ethical. Shade was a topnotch hacker and a class act. "Is she in trouble?" Kit's question confirmed she knew Shade. But if he knew about Shade, he knew too much already. Theirs was a small and discreet community.

"She's safe, but she sent me because she is worried about you. Problems are coming your way."

Kit wasn't interested in a cloak-and-dagger routine. "I don't do that type of work anymore. I work for a florist. If Shade was worried about me, she would have sent me a message directly." Online. Over the phone. Sending a messenger did not seem like Shade's style.

"You've been hard to find."

Her pride flooded through her. At least she hadn't made it painfully easy for her enemies to locate her. Shade was a friend, but to keep herself safe, she'd had to hide from everyone, and that had meant creating a new online identity. "Yet here you are," Kit said, wondering how he had located her. If he had found her, then her enemies could, as well.

"I went through a lot of trouble to locate you. Thousands in bribes, hours on stakeouts and hacking the United States' civilian records," he said.

The records the government kept to allow them to track almost anyone. Library cards, credit card bills and facial recognition from streaming video feeds made hiding next to impossible. Kit had believed knowing how the government could track her meant she could be untraceable. She had been mistaken.

"Coming for you in person allows us to protect you."

"Us?" She looked around. She could spot a military man from fifty paces. This man had the look of someone with service experience, but no one else jumped out at her.

"I work with a team, but I am here alone."

"You work for Shade?" she asked.

"With her," he said.

He didn't like to be submissive. Definitely military. "I'm fine here. My family is close, and if you haven't noticed, my sister hired a dozen security guards for this party."

The man arched a brow. "Your family and some guards for hire can't protect you. You have dangerous enemies."

"Maybe you're one of them," she said. She lifted her phone to snap his picture. He snatched it from her hands before she could capture his image and send it with an SOS to her safety net, a list of computer hackers who would take his picture to the authorities if anything happened to her.

"I've heard a computer in your hands is as dangerous as a weapon."

A compliment. "You heard right. I'll do what's needed to protect myself and my family."

"Like calling in an air strike?" he asked, sounding amused.

"That was a joke," she said. When she had been on the project years ago, she had ordered an air strike against a general who had pissed her off. She'd known the military had safeguards to prevent friendly fire, but it had been a clear warning not to screw with her.

"Not everyone is amused by your sense of humor," he said.

"I've been told it's a little warped. Give me my phone."

He handed it to her. "I need to take you somewhere safe."

He could be a wolf in sheep's clothing. If he had found her and knew about Shade, he could be masquerading as friendly but working with her enemies. "I can protect myself." Or at least, she could run and disappear.

The music stopped dead, and the lanterns and bar lights on the rooftop flickered before going out completely. Kit glanced at her phone, confused to see the red warning icon that she had no cell service. Panic flared, and she sensed something bad was unfolding.

He said, "Not from—"

The rat-tat-tat of gunfire cut him off. The man grabbed Kit and held her against him, sheltering her with his body and forcing her to the ground.

Screaming and the sound of glass breaking filled the air. The gunfire meant that her life, and the lives of her family and people around her, were in danger. The strength and power of the stranger holding her against him was weirdly comforting. She felt a gun at his side. And another one. And a knife in a leather sheath.

"Please stop that," he said.

She stilled her hands. "Are you wearing a vest?"

"Of course I am," he said, reaching for one of his weapons and shoving her behind him. He pivoted on his heels while staying in a squat.

Lights from adjacent buildings, the moon and the city below were the only illumination.

A man with a large gun swung it in a wide circle around him, eliciting more squeals of fear and pleading. Two others were at his sides. They wore clear plastic masks, distorting their faces, and black clothes. Between their disguises and the darkness, Kit couldn't tell anything about these men.

"We're looking for a woman. If you stay calm, no one will be hurt. Kit Walker, come forward or we'll kill every person on this roof."

Kit tried to push the man off her. He didn't budge.

"Stay down. I will get you out of this."

"Not at the expense of everyone here." Kit couldn't see her mother's, sister's or brother's face, but she guessed they were terrified and confused. She was the nobody in the family. They must have been wondering who would barge into a party, armed, and attempt to kidnap her.

He stood, jerking her to her feet, turning her to protect her with his body and bringing a gun to her temple. "If you want her, you'll have to fight me for her."

He had lied. He was here to hurt her.

Every person on the roof was looking at them. Her mother screamed. Marissa was pointing from her bodyguards to Kit, perhaps begging them to do something. Kit tried to pull free. Including the one holding her, four madmen were after her. How far would she get, especially in these shoes?

She had known her history would catch up with her. She had been warned that she couldn't walk away from the Locker and start over as if nothing had happened, as if she hadn't been key in creating a system that protected the United States and threatened other countries in subversive and catastrophic ways.

But darned if she hadn't tried.

The liar dragged her through the crowd, gun poking her. "Shoot anyone and she dies," the liar said to the man at the door.

Party guests were cowered on the ground. The shooting had stopped.

If she made it out of here, the liar would probably kill her when he realized she wouldn't work as a traitor to the United States. She was worth more alive than dead, and that would buy her some time. She had refused to take part in the training about resisting advanced interrogation techniques, aka torture, but now she wished she was prepared. How stiff-lipped would she be when her loyalty to America was put to the test?

Kit had made bad choices in her professional career. Being involved with the Locker was the worst. One of the lead computer scientists on the project had suffered a stroke. The stress and the deadlines had gotten to him. The engineer who had masterminded the Locker had experienced a complete break with reality. He had behaved strangely for weeks, and then he had snapped. Both men had been removed from the project. It had been devastating for Kit personally, and the professional pressure on her had increased. She had worried that she would become ill, either physically or mentally, but she had held it together. Looking back, her naïveté had saved her. She hadn't fully grasped the enemies she was making or the importance of her work.

"We can make an arrangement. We'll pay double your fee," the man with the assault rifle said. He had a mustache. She didn't trust men with mustaches.

"Let's take this downstairs." That gravelly voice commanded respect. Kit wondered if she could get free of him. In movies and TV, spunky heroines broke away with a well-placed kick. But his grip on her was firm, and he was probably a very good shot. A man who owned a bulletproof vest wasn't a novice with a weapon. How far could she get before being gunned down?

The liar dragged her into the stairwell, where there were fewer witnesses. Where were the police? Had they been called? The signal on her phone had gone out, but could someone else have contacted the authorities? Could they help her?

The probability of her dying was high, and Kit didn't have much to lose. He could shoot her on the stairs and then throw her body down fifteen flights. She had a slim chance of surviving that. She would run the first chance she had.

"If you shoot me, make sure I'm dead before you toss my body down the stairs," she said.

"What?" he asked. He sounded annoyed. She

didn't care if he was annoyed. If she had to die, she wanted some say in the matter.

"I don't want to be paralyzed and brain-dead and a huge problem for my family while I'm in a vegetative state. Shoot to kill. Navy SEAL me—you know, one to the heart and one to the head."

He swore under his breath. "Please just shut up."

The other three men followed them down the stairs. They wanted to bring her in alive. The liar might want her dead. She was better off with the people who wanted her alive. At least it would buy her an opportunity to escape.

Though he was holding her firmly, he wasn't hurting her or jerking her around. He was almost carrying her down the stairs. When they reached the ground floor, they stepped into the narrow alley between the buildings.

"If you're prepared to pay me, then I'm prepared to give her to you," the liar said.

A mercenary with no moral compass except one that pointed to the highest dollar amount. What a loser. She revoked her good thoughts about how attractive he was and replaced the word *attractive* with *louse*.

"Tell me the routing and account number and the money is yours," the other man said.

The liar shouted out a series of numbers. Kit memorized them. If she escaped him, she would rob him blind. He would make a very, very large and untraceable donation to St. Jude Children's Research Hospital.

The mercenary put his gun in the hand holding her and took out his phone to confirm the money transfer had been made. The distraction could be a chance to run for freedom. She struggled against him, but his arm was unmovable. She elbowed him in the gut and hit only his vest and the muscle beneath. He didn't flinch or make any noise of pain. At least that would have given her some satisfaction.

"Thanks for the payout," he said. "Trust me," he whispered into her ear before he pushed her to the other men.

She stumbled in her heels, but one of the men grabbed her. He dragged her toward a car at the opening of the alley.

More gunshots, and Kit ducked. Were they killing the mercenary? It would serve him right. Would-be murderers had it coming.

A man with curly hair shoved her against the car and pulled her to the ground. He wasn't moving, and he was heavy. It was hard to breathe with his weight pinning her. Several seconds passed before she realized he was dead on top of her. She kicked at him, trying to move him off her. Now was her opportunity to run for freedom.

The body gave way, and then the mercenary was hauling her to her feet. The other men were dead in the alley, blood pooling around their bodies.

Hysteria and panic clawed at her. If he would callously kill these men, he would kill her. Three more men entered the alley. They advanced on her and the mercenary. He nudged her farther down the alley in the opposite direction.

He was already shooting at the others. "Run, Princess. Get out of here."

Confusion morphed into self-preservation. He was letting her go. She started to run and then stopped to look over her shoulder. He was fighting the three men, landing punches but taking punches, too. She wanted to run, but something held her feet in place.

Before she could decide what to do next, the mercenary had knocked out the three men. He raced toward her. "Come on. I told you to run. You need a better sense of survival."

"I was worried about you," she said.

He grunted. "Don't worry about me. Focus your energy on living through this."

He threw her on the back of a motorcycle and then climbed on. He handed her a helmet. She didn't have it snapped and he was already taking off from the alley. As the cycle lurched, she grabbed his shoulders to steady herself.

She had too many questions. Was he planning to sell her or kill her? He had already sold her, but then had saved her. Why? What did he need her to do? What was his connection to the Locker?

The motorcycle drew to a stop on the side of a quiet street lined with boutiques closed for the night. Kit's legs were shaking with fatigue, and her body was trembling.

He helped her off the motorcycle and she collapsed against him, unable to stand. Her dress was torn and dirty, and based on the way it was twisted, she must have looked indecent. She'd lost a shoe, and her foot hurt.

"I think there's something in my heel," she said, lifting it and trying to get a better look.

He set her on his motorcycle and knelt on the ground. Though his gaze dodged left and right, he examined her foot with surprising gentleness. "A piece of glass is in it."

"Pull it out," she said.

He held up his finger and reached into a bag on his bike. He removed a first aid kit. "Your shoe is the most impractical choice."

"I wasn't planning to run away from armed killers tonight," she said.

She flinched when he removed the glass. Then he squeezed her foot and cleaned it with alcohol wipes. She held her teeth together to keep from screaming.

"It's not too deep. We'll have a doctor look at it later."

What were his plans for her? If he took her to a doctor, could she find help? "Why did you save me?"

"I was sent to retrieve you."

"You sold me to those men."

He gave her a look that said, "Get real." "I conned them out of two-point-five million dollars."

"Aren't you worried they'll find you?" she asked. That was a lot of money to lose. Retribution would be paid.

"No."

Just *no*? Not worried about it? Who was this man?

She had left this confusing world years before with zero intention of returning. She hadn't fit in then, and she didn't fit in now. It had rules she didn't understand. "Please let me go," she said.

Compassion touched the corners of his eyes. "I didn't plan for it to go this way."

What had he planned? He'd shown up wearing two guns, a knife and a bulletproof vest. He had to have expected bullets would fly and people would be hurt. "What are we doing now?" They couldn't wait on the street long. People were looking for them.

"We're close to the safe house. Someone will explain more then."

"You can't explain now?" she asked.

"No."

He was infuriating with his uninformative responses.

"I need to call in that I have you."

Call in to whom? "What if I run?" she asked.

"You don't want to do that," he said.

Yes, she did.

"If you run, I will catch you. You are in danger, and it's my job to take you somewhere safe. The sooner you accept that you need my help, the easier this will go."

As a retrieval specialist for the West Company and as a former member of the Special Forces Operational Detachment-Delta, Griffin Brooks knew not every extraction went well. During his time with

Delta Force and then with the West Company, he could count on one hand the number that had.

This case was especially problematic. He was part of a team locating the group that had worked on a secret government project. Those individuals were being hunted by an extremist organization, and when the scientists didn't comply with the terrorists' demands, they were killed and their bodies dumped in various locations around the United States. The West Company had kept the murders, and any connection between them, quiet and out of the media. As the bodies piled up, the United States government became more nervous. They wanted this handled quickly and effectively.

The international terrorist group known as Incognito had started out as a cyber-only terrorist organization. In recent months, they had allied themselves with several mercenary groups and had shifted their focus to collecting the scientists who had worked on the Locker. Their means were no longer isolated to the computer. Kidnappings and murders were frequently tied to them. Griffin didn't know what the Locker was, but it was important to keep it, and by extension the scientists who had contributed to it, safe. He knew the code names for three team members who were considered most at risk: Kit, who had gone by the name Lotus, Arsenic, and Stargazer. Arsenic and Stargazer had left the project before it had ended and were proving harder to trace.

Incognito was hunting the three lead scientists, and they wouldn't stop. The United States had connected the dead bodies to the secret military project, and they'd called in the West Company to assist. Details were closely guarded, and every item was need-to-know.

Connor West, owner of the West Company, had deployed other specialists to retrieve the remaining members of the project, beyond the three leads. Some were deep in hiding. Griffin had been assigned the task to locate and bring in Kit Walker. He had studied her file, but she was more than a techie with a PhD and a love of computers. He had expected her to be smart, but he hadn't expected her spunk or the red minidress and sky-high bedroom heels.

Dress and shoes aside, she wasn't his type. Since his wife had died, he went for women who had looks over brains and were more submissive than bold. Griffin enjoyed the company of women, and he liked for them to play along with his desires. Being in control in the bedroom was a turn-on for him. Nothing wrong with that if the woman was willing. He was lucky that plenty were. He wasn't lonely for company when he wanted it. Given what he did for a living, he wasn't looking for long-term. He'd had that with Beth, and though it had been amazing, he wouldn't find it twice in one lifetime.

Griffin dialed Connor on his secure line. While he spoke, Kit rubbed her arms and looked around. Was she thinking of running? He would catch her. If he had to bring her in wounded, it was better than bringing her in dead. She wouldn't get far on her injured foot. He'd bandaged it, but any pressure and it would resume bleeding.

She shivered again, and he removed the sweatshirt from his motorcycle trunk and tossed it to her. She smiled at him gratefully and pulled it over her dress. The shirt was long on her, falling below the hemline of her dress. He was momentarily fixated on her pair of slim, toned legs.

Her legs weren't her best feature, though. Her best feature was her eyes. He could get lost in their depths. He could see so much going on behind them. He liked that. He liked it a lot.

"Get her to the safe house. I'll send a computer as soon as I can," Connor said.

"Right. A computer." Connor's wife Kate, also known as Shade, had reasoned that Kit would be more comfortable and possibly of use to them in the immediate future with a computer in her hands.

Kit drew the hood of his sweatshirt up, and Griffin smiled. It worked on her. She had a sexy nerd look, her hair wild around her shoulders and her lips twisted in annoyance.

He wrapped up his call and disconnected. "Ready?" he asked her.

She glared at him from under the hood. "If I run, you'd have to chase me."

"That's right."

"But you don't want to hurt me."

He didn't want to hurt her. But if he had to tackle her, he would. "I will do what I need to bring you in."

Chapter 2

She was going to run. Her muscles clenched. Her history with the Locker hadn't indicated that she'd had deception training. In his line of work, Griffin expected liars. Kit was a refreshing change of pace.

Kit made it two steps before he caught her and pushed her against the brick wall of a nearby building. He exercised control as he held her wrists in his. He wasn't looking to break her arms.

"You're hurting me." He loosened his grip. She pulled her arm free and punched him in the face.

It barely registered. He'd been struck harder—much harder—before. Tonight, even. "We need to work on your self-defense skills."

Her mouth trembled. Her eyes welled with tears. Was she going to cry? He shouldn't care if she did.

"Let me go, brute."

Brute? He had been called a lot of names, but never that. "Will you run?" he asked.

She shook her head. "I know you'll catch me. But I won't stop trying to get away from you."

"You won't have to deal with me for much longer. After I drop you off, you're someone else's headache." Maybe someone else could get through to her that she was in danger and needed protecting.

They walked back to his motorcycle, and she kicked it over. He looked at her in surprise. "Don't like the bike?"

"Look at me. How do you think I feel right now?"

"I have no idea how you feel." Angry, clearly. He righted the bike.

She folded her arms over her chest. "So that part of you is broken. You kill people and you manhandle me. You don't care how I feel."

"I am not paid to care how you feel. I am paid to keep you safe. How is your foot?"

"It hurts."

"I'll help you onto the seat," he said. He lifted her in his arms.

"Everyone can see up my dress," she said, squirming in his arms, trying to tug it and the sweatshirt down.

"There's no one here," he said.

"I'm never wearing a dress again," she said.

He liked her determination and gave her credit for attempting to flee. "You look good in it."

"It's a designer dress," she said.

"Whatever it is, it's nice."

"My sister bought it for me," she said.

"You may have to explain why it's damaged," he said.

She rolled her eyes. "Please. She couldn't care less. She has a closet full of dresses, and this one is four sizes too big for her."

Her sister was supermodel Marissa Walker. Marissa had been on the cover of some sports magazines in a swimsuit and had traveled the world. Rare for two sisters to have such extraordinarily different talents.

"Are you thinking about sleeping with my sister now?" Kit asked.

He hadn't been. "Are you thinking about me sleeping with your sister?"

"Don't be gross."

Not much about Marissa Walker was gross, but imagining a sibling with a lover was. "You brought it up."

"I'm trying to figure you out," she said. She touched the side of his face and then his ear, running her finger down the curve of it.

He turned his head. "Stop that."

"You're bruised, and your ear is bleeding," she said.

His ears were ringing, but they would stop. "I'll look at it later."

He helped her onto the bike and then mounted it. It was a short distance to the safe house. He circled the block twice, ensuring he wasn't followed. The safe house was a temporary holdover for the night.

Kit would change hands many times to lose any trail connecting her to her final destination: a supersecret military base. Griffin hadn't been told the location. From what he'd understood, few knew it existed.

Five more minutes and he could finish this job. Kit was alive, and that was how he would remember her. The beautiful, feisty hacker in the red dress. When he stopped in front of the safe house, he helped Kit off the bike and let her lean on him as they took the stairs to the back door.

Kit removed the sweatshirt and extended her hand to him.

"Keep it," he said. He didn't need it and she seemed to be more comfortable having it.

"Thank you," she said. She knotted the sleeves around her waist.

He knocked once on the door, and it opened a couple of inches. "It is a truth universally acknowledged..." the voice said.

Griffin finished the quote. "...that a single man in possession of a good fortune, must be in want of a wife."

He guessed Kate had picked the quote. Since she and Connor had married and were starting a family, she believed that their operatives were destined for the same happiness. Griffin had tried to tell her that happiness came in many packages, not all of them involving a spouse and children.

Griffin's life had been made better by a woman, but most relationships ended with deep unhappiness.

Even Beth, whom he had loved with his whole being, had broken his heart when she'd died.

The door opened all the way.

He set Kit across the threshold. "She needs shoes. She has an injury to her foot, and a doctor should look at it."

The man inside nodded. Griffin didn't recognize him, but he didn't know every operative in Connor's network. "I'll take care of it."

"Good luck to you," he said to Kit.

She nodded once, sadly. "Goodbye, brute."

She didn't know his name, but by this point, it didn't matter. It was probably better that she knew nothing about him. He didn't want her searching for him via the internet and exacting revenge. Griffin sincerely hoped she would realize she was in danger and he had only been trying to help her.

"Don't be a flight risk," he said.

She stared at him. "Can you make sure my family is okay?"

It wasn't part of the job, but he couldn't say no. "I'll check in."

"Will you get me a message if anything is wrong?"

He nodded once. "My boss will know where you are."

As he returned to his motorcycle, he couldn't drive away. Leaving her bothered him. He didn't get emotionally tied to his missions and he felt connected to her. Usually, he didn't think about people he worked with past the ending of a mission. Emotions had no place in his world.

It was her eyes. They were the most expressive eyes.

He started his bike and then a small detail, one easily overlooked, hit him. A sick feeling swamped him and he instinctively checked his gun.

It suddenly registered that the man who had greeted them at the door had had a tattoo on his neck. A spear tattoo that was a sign of Incognito.

With the press of a button, Griffin sent an alert to Connor to let him know the mission was not going according to plan. Griffin was up the back stairs in seconds. He kicked in the door and rushed inside. They could have slit her throat. Left her for dead. Any horrible ending could have befallen her, and it would be because of his mistake.

An image of Beth flashed to mind, her dead body lying on sterile metal in a morgue, and Griffin fought to control the sadness and anger. Beth's death was why he didn't work protective detail. He was best at extractions. He couldn't keep his wife safe. How would he keep a stranger safe?

"Kit!" he called, panic rising inside him. The panic drove him, sharpening every sense.

Silence. They had already fled the house with her or killed her. He heard a car engine outside.

Griffin cursed his stupidity and raced for his motorcycle. He climbed onto it. A navy sedan was driving down the street, and hanging out of the closed trunk of the car was his sweatshirt.

They had Kit in the trunk of the car. She had to be alive. He wouldn't accept that she had been killed. Incognito wanted her alive, and they had no way to know if she would cooperate yet. From what he knew of the other victims, it had been several days from the time they went missing to the time their bodies had been found. No explanation given. The West Company suspected they had been punished for not providing the answers Incognito wanted. They had been loyal and had kept their mouths shut about the Locker.

Kit could be destined for that same fate. She knew more than most about the project. The other two leads on the project were insane and medically incapacitated, and the West Company was searching for them, as well. That left Kit in the hot seat.

Griffin raced after them. His bike caught up to the car. A man leaned out of the back of the car and shot at him. He swerved his bike. He couldn't return fire at this distance. He couldn't risk Kit getting hurt.

He sped ahead of the car and then slammed to a stop thirty yards past the sedan. He pivoted and pulled his gun, aiming at the driver's head. A trained sniper, he could make the shot, but he could also be hit head-on by the car as it veered out of control.

One shot. Two. Clean through the head. The car skidded and crashed into a vehicle parked on the side of the road. If Kit was hurt...

Leaving his bike, Griffin ran to the car. He killed the other two men in the vehicle before they could exit, their punishment for kidnapping Kit.

He opened the driver's side door, shoving the dead man to the side, and popped the trunk.

He lifted a very frightened Kit from the back of the car.

She was shaking and had a welt on her head. "Did you see the sweatshirt?"

An intentional message and a sign of her faith in him. "I did see it. That was quick thinking."

"I hoped you would realize they were bad," she said, curling her arms around his body and laying her head on his chest.

A strange sensation swept over him. He didn't hug people in the field, but Kit needed him. He didn't pull away.

"Did they say anything to you?" he asked.

"They want me to break into a system I built," she said.

That was in line with what the West Company knew of their motives. "I know."

"I can't. I don't think anyone understands. When we built that system, it was not hackable. It is not hackable. Even by the people who built it. We designed it to be unalterable and uncontrollable by any one person. It's intelligently designed world-class technology. It changes with cybersecurity advancements and keeps pace with new viruses and exploitations without human intervention. Who is planning to hack the Locker?" Kit asked.

"Incognito."

She drew her eyebrows together. "Oh. I'm familiar with their processes and their attacks in the cyber world. But how is Incognito finding people who worked on the project? We used code names, and our real names were never to be revealed."

"Looks like something went wrong. Someone somewhere made the connection," he said.

"Bank payouts. Initial hiring documents. That data was supposed to be destroyed," Kit said, terror in her eyes.

Griffin understood the fear. He had underestimated Incognito and Kit had almost paid with her life.

Kit had voluntarily spent a year of her life confined to an underground military base. She was familiar with their processes and protocols, but she didn't want to return to a military base of any kind. The fake lights they had used to replace sunlight, the restrictions and the sense of being closed in had been persistent. Kit had needed to lie a lot that year, too. She had told her family she was traveling overseas and couldn't return home. Her sister offering to pay for her flight or to fly out to visit her had been brutal to turn down. It was as if Marissa had known something was amiss and had wanted to confirm.

Kit had first been recruited to work on the Locker out of graduate school. The project had sounded exciting: build a cybersecurity supercomputer, working with the most advanced technology and the world's best computer scientists and engineers. It had seemed like a great opportunity. But the reality of being cut off from the outside world had worn on her. The work had kept her busy seven days a week, but she had been depressed.

Her rescuer had received instructions and had taken her to a military base. As the copter landed, it was pitch-black outside. Without her phone, she was disoriented about the time and place.

"This is the safest place Connor could arrange on short notice," Brute said.

Kit stayed tucked close to Brute. Her brain hadn't caught up to the events of the night yet. She was physically tired, but her thoughts were racing. "Where are we?"

"I can't tell you," Brute said.

"I'll figure it out," she said. Eventually. Would she be confined for long? Would Brute leave her? A couple of hours ago, being away from him was all she wanted. Now she was filled with fear. Men were gunning for her, and a classified project was no longer a secret. How many people knew?

They disembarked the copter and ran across the tarmac to a nondescript tan building.

"We won't be here long. This is a stopover until more secure arrangements can be made," Brute said.

"We? You're staying with me?" she asked. It was a relief to hear.

"My orders have changed. Until my boss can find someone to take over for me, you're stuck with me."

Being stuck with him sounded good, too good. It dawned on her that she was developing a crush on her kidnapper. Or had he saved her? Kit didn't know how to judge him. He was working with the military, but that in itself didn't mean he was to be trusted or that he was one of the good guys.

Two men in army fatigues escorted them to a sparsely furnished room with two cots and barred windows high on the walls. The walls were gray, but not in a supertrendy, freshly renovated way. In a dull, depressing, covering cinder blocks way. At least the room was not underground.

The fatigues worn by their escorts were her first clue to where she was. An army base within a twenty-minute copter ride from the Los Angeles area.

"Can I get a change of clothes?" she asked. Her dress was torn, dirty and uncomfortable. She was cold and longed for sweatpants to match the hoodie Brute had given her.

"You hate that dress, don't you?" he asked.

"I feel like a stuffed sausage."

"You don't look like one," he said.

It was something. The compliment made it hard to stay mad at Brute, especially given that he had saved her twice that day. He had a gruff manner, but he was looking out for her. Without him, where would she be? In the hands of Incognito, no doubt.

"I'd love something comfortable and warm," she said. What they'd have access to would be limited, but they could issue her a pair of military sweats.

"She also needs shoes and a doctor," he said.

The men saluted and left to acquire the items they had requested, she hoped.

Her foot was throbbing mildly. "I almost forgot about my foot."

"Let me look at it."

She sat on one of the cots, and he knelt on the floor in front of her, setting her foot on his knee. "It doesn't look good. Needs to be cleaned and dressed."

He propped her foot on the cot and took a seat on the other one. He looked tired. The red welt on his face was turning a pale yellow. He was unbearably handsome with his piercing green eyes and the slight cleft in his chin. His steely demeanor was contradicted by the warmth in his eyes.

"Are you in pain?" she asked.

He rolled his neck, stretching his spine. "It's manageable."

What level of pain would be unmanageable for him? She had worked with military men who had seemed incapable of registering pain. What about the injuries she couldn't see?

The soldiers returned with a stack of the requested supplies, and a medic entered the room behind them.

The medic examined her foot. "This needs to be cleaned," he said. "I'll take you to the infirmary."

Kit stood, the pain shooting up her leg. She winced. Brute stood from his cot and lifted her into his arms as if carrying her across a threshold. "Lead the way, Doc."

The medic brought them to a brightly lit room with a patient bed in the middle and medical supplies on the shelves around them. The process of cleaning her foot was excruciating. Kit wanted to cry, yet Brute had to have worse injuries, and he seemed calm. She thought of something else, something other than the pain in her heel.

She couldn't watch the medic work so she stared at Brute. He was looking at her foot, but he lifted his gaze and their eyes met.

He intrigued her. More than muscle and brawn, he was smart. Not smart in a nerdy, tech-savvy way, but he was definitely street-smart, taking in details. Despite the intense time they had spent together, Kit didn't know his name. When she had worked on the Locker, she had been trained not to ask names or for details of someone's life. This man knew Shade. She hadn't been active online in the circles where Kit floated, and internet rumors indicated Shade had gone to work for a white hat organization. Had Shade gone to work for the same company Griffin worked for?

The medic was applying ointment and bandaging her heel. "You'll need to take it easy on your foot. Try to stay off it and give it a chance to heal. After you bathe, put on a fresh bandage." He handed a box of bandages and tape to Brute.

She hopped off the table and held up her hand as Brute approached. "I can walk. It feels much better." It didn't. It was aching. At least she had the confidence that it was clean and treated.

After walking for a few minutes, Kit gripped Brute's arm, using him like a cane. They were escorted back to their small room.

When they were alone, she sat on the cot, propping up her foot. "Could I use a phone to find out how my family is?"

"No direct contact. We don't know whose phones have been compromised. I'll call and request information on your family," he said.

"When can I talk to them?" she asked. She wanted

reassurance they were safe and unharmed in the melee.

"Not yet."

"Who do you work for?" she asked.

"I work for the West Company."

Kit inhaled. She had heard of them. Never met or worked with one of their operatives—at least, as far as she knew. After another secret government spy organization had crumbled under corruption and criminal charges, Kit had heard rumors that the West Company had taken over for the defunct agency.

Of course, it wasn't like the West Company had a website, and government officials denied its existence. Before now, Kit had only read rumors about it.

"Shade works for them?" Kit asked.

"Shade is married to the head of the West Company," Brute said.

"Why are you telling me this?" she asked.

"I've been authorized to explain this to you. We want to earn your trust. Taking you from your sister's birthday party probably didn't go a long way to winning you over," Brute said. "We haven't decided how we'll spin your disappearance. It's already hit the news, thanks to your sister's fame."

When Kit had worked on the Locker, contact with her family had been limited and controlled and monitored. Kit had felt like a prisoner. The precautions were for her safety, but they had felt like chains around her neck.

Her family would be worried about her, but they would forgive her. She would be released soon. The government couldn't keep her here against her will. She had a life. Her work at the florist. Her apartment. Her online life. Why did that now depress her? No one except her mother, brother, sister and boss would have known she had gone missing.

Brute dialed his phone and checked in with someone, presumably at the West Company, and then handed her the phone. "Connor West is the lead of the West Company. He is on the line and available to answer questions."

Kit took the phone from him, feeling a mix of awe and disbelief. "This is Kit Walker."

"Is there anything we can get for you?" Connor asked. Behind the strength in his voice, she heard kindness.

She didn't require much, and she would be home soon. "I want to know if my family is safe. I want to be informed as the situation changes."

"They are safe and I will let you know if anything changes. I've assigned an operative to each of your family members to ensure their safety while we work on this situation," Connor said.

"What will you tell my family about me?" Kit asked. She didn't want to put them through any stress.

"We're discussing our strategy. Your family knows you're safe. We want your family to be reassured, but we don't want to alert the men looking for you that you're alive or give clues to your whereabouts."

When she had left the Locker project, she had known this was a possibility. She had signed and agreed to so many rules and disclosures and confidentiality statements making it clear that despite her precautions, her future was in jeopardy. She had made an effort to put distance between herself and the Locker, but apparently not enough.

She wrapped up the call. She had no control over the situation. No phone, no computer, no access to the outside world, and she hated it.

She could at least make herself more comfortable. She pointed to the clothes that had been brought for her. "Please turn around so I can change."

He did as she asked, giving her his back. "Do I have to worry that you'll attack me?"

"Are you making fun of me?" she asked. How would she attack him?

"Not in the least. I'm trying to understand you."

"You pretended to like me at my sister's party," she said, thinking of how he had approached her. "Were you trying to seduce me?"

"I was trying to convince you to leave the party with me so I could take you somewhere safe."

It felt great to peel off the dress, but she didn't want to return the hoodie. It smelled of him and that made her feel safe. She slipped on the military sweat pants and T-shirt. "How did that work out for you?" she asked, adjusting the drawstrings on her pants.

"You're alive, aren't you?" he asked.

"That's one way to look at it," she said.

"Any day I wake up is a blessing," Brute said.

An odd statement, but perhaps coming from a West Company operative who had spent hours in dangerous locations, it was his truth. "What exactly do you do for the West Company?" she asked.

"Retrieval specialist," he replied.

Deciding she could do what she wanted, she pulled on the hoodie. When someone gave her a computer, she would give up the hoodie. Maybe.

"How did they pick you?" she asked.

"Excuse me?"

"How did they know I would find you attractive? Was there an assessment done on me, a written profile?" Having worked for the government, she knew that complex plans were thought through on many levels—psychological, emotional and physical. The government had her profile, and they knew what made her tick. That knowledge made her suspicious of everything they said and did to her. Was Brute playing a role? How much of his behavior was him and how much an act to manipulate her?

"Do you always say what's on your mind?" he asked.

Kit refused to be cowed. "I'm trying to assess my situation so I can understand how to get out of this."

"You can't get out of it unless you want to be taken prisoner by Incognito and then killed," Brute said.

"Don't try to scare me," she said. "I might be weak now, but if I can get my hands on a computer, I will rain missiles down on you."

He faced her and smiled again. She had to get over that smile. It shouldn't have rattled her.

"If you rain missiles down on me, then you'll be

raining missiles down on you, because we're attached at the hip."

That knowledge surprised her. "I thought you were handing me off at the first opportunity," she said.

"I'll release you when I know you are safe," he said.

His words touched her. "Why does it matter what happens to me?"

Confusion darted across his face. "I swore to do a job. I will do that job."

She had known him for less than a day and he felt responsible for her. "You have integrity. Do you also have a name you're willing to share with me?"

"Griffin."

She hadn't expected a full name, but at least she could think of him as something other than brute. The longer they were together, the less she thought of him as a bully or a kidnapper. "Wings of an eagle and body of a lion."

"That's the one," he said.

"Is that your name, or is it another ploy to manipulate me psychologically?"

Griffin appeared flabbergasted. "Though it may seem otherwise to you, this was a well-thought-out operation with considerably less time spent analyzing you and more time spent countering the threats against you. I was not selected to seduce you or manipulate you."

Her cheeks grew hot. "That's good, because I am not easily seduced." Most men didn't try. She didn't exude sex appeal and confidence the way her sister did.

"That red dress was made for a woman who was looking for sex."

She blinked at him. Maybe Marissa had been right and that dress had looked good on her. She hadn't felt sexy in it. "I wasn't looking for anything. My sister wanted me to wear the dress and it was her birthday, so I indulged her." But she didn't want to discuss her insecurities or Marissa's beauty. "What now?"

Griffin pulled his cot across the door. "We sleep while we can."

Chapter 3

The squeaks of the cot springs gave away that Kit wasn't asleep. She was tossing and turning.

"Why aren't you sleeping?" Griffin asked. His cot wasn't the most comfortable, but he had slept on worse. At least he was dry and no one was shooting at him.

Kit shifted in her bed. She was the most restless sleeper he had ever been in the same room with. "How do you know I'm not?"

"For one, you answered me. For two, your breathing is irregular and the noises of your cot indicate movement."

She blew out her breath. "I'm upset. It's been an upsetting day. I'm worried about my family."

The West Company would ensure their safety. She

had nothing to worry about in that regard. "They are being guarded."

She let out a harrumph. He should have stayed quiet, but he hadn't been sleeping, either. He wouldn't give in to the exhaustion that pulled at the corners of his brain until he was sure she was asleep.

"Let me call my mom."

A security breach to allow direct contact. "Can't happen. People are looking for you. We can't risk someone tracing the call or your mom alerting anyone to your status."

He could envision Kit glaring at him in the dark.

"Do you think I don't understand how to mask where a call is coming from? I know to think before I speak. I have not questioned how well you do your job, snatching people and punching people, and I'm asking you to trust me to do this."

She didn't strike him as an overconfident woman, and he guessed she could back up her statement. "I don't have permission to give you a phone." They were working on obtaining a secure computer and phone for her.

"I am not a prisoner. I am a person," Kit said.

Griffin turned on the overhead light to look at her. "I know you are a person. A person I am trying to keep safe." He was having enough trouble wrapping his mind around the idea that he was responsible for protecting her. His complex about that was a twisted mess. He had accepted the assignment to retrieve her and deliver her to a safe house. This added complexity caused uncertainties to surface.

"Give me your phone," she said.

"You can't call your family and check in. We want your whereabouts to remain unknown to Incognito." Since that wasn't dissuading her, he decided to tell her the brutal truth. "If anyone knows that you contacted your family, that family member will be tortured for information. Do you understand what torture is?"

She glared at him. "I am aware of what it is."

"Have you ever been tortured?" He hated pressing her, but he needed her to understand the severity of what was playing out.

"Not physically."

He considered her words. "If you want to check the internet for news about the incident at your sister's party, I'll allow it, but no underhanded stuff."

"Underhanded stuff?" She seemed pleased at the small victory.

"You know what I mean. No sending secret, encrypted messages. It's a point, click and read-only venture."

She smiled. "Thank you. That will help me sleep. I need to see for myself."

He crossed to her cot and sat next to her. She moved away and extended her hand for the phone. He shook his head. "I watch what you are doing, every finger motion."

She rolled her eyes. "You are an untrusting man."

"That is a trait that will keep you alive." He handed her his phone. Activity on it was monitored by Kate West. If Kit tried to pull anything, Kate would know it.

Kit smelled of the beach. It was an odd smell to associate with someone, warm sand and the waves, when she hadn't been near the shore. She elbowed him. "You're too close. You're crowding me."

"The screen is small."

"Is that a tattoo on your neck?" she asked. She traced a finger over the tattoo that ran from the base of his neck along his collarbone and to his biceps.

"Yes."

He didn't lean away from her touch, knowing the slightest distance would give her fingers time to do mischief on his phone. Her profile was fresh in his mind. When it came to computers and technology, she was not to be underestimated.

"Can I see the whole tattoo?" she asked.

"You want me to take my shirt off?"

"Yes."

"When you're done with the phone." She'd use the time he had the fabric over his eyes to send a message.

Her frown told him he was right. The short time he'd spent with her, he'd learned at least that. Genius behind a computer, but she had no game face. Everything she felt and thought played out in her expression.

She clicked a few links, read an article and then handed him the phone. "No mention of anyone being killed. Except the men who broke into the party, and I already knew what happened to them. I'm surprised the reporter didn't include a quote from my sister expressing her grief about me going missing. No mention of me missing at all."

"You sound angry about that," Griffin said, slipping his phone back into his pocket.

"Not angry. Resigned. For as long as I can remember, Marissa has been at the center of a three-ring circus, and I've been the person selling popcorn to the crowd."

"Does it bother you to have a famous sister?"

She shrugged. "It bothers me when people make comparisons between us. If my sister had been average-looking, then the fact that I'm below average wouldn't stand out so much."

She had a low opinion of her looks. He found her tremendously appealing. Griffin didn't go for stick-thin and expressionless, a look he had associated with her sister and a number of guests at the party. "You are not below average."

Kit stared at him, her eyes wide. "If you're making fun of me, stop it."

"I'm not joking with you. I'm speaking plainly."

"Then I can speak plainly and tell you that you are a handsome man. You're scary, but I don't think you're planning to hurt me." A question on the end of the statement.

He had killed to protect her. He had placed himself at great risk to keep her safe. If he had wanted to hurt her, she'd be dead. He had sworn to Connor that he would stay with Kit until his job was complete. He would do what he could to protect her, and that had deep meaning to him. Connor was aware of

Griffin's lack of experience in this arena and what had happened to Beth. "I won't hurt you."

"I believe that. Of course, I've believed a lot of things that have turned out to be lies."

The hurt in her words was heavy. Griffin wasn't privy to the details of her personal life. "We won't be together long, but while we are, you can count on me to be honest with you."

"What if someone comes in here to kill me?" she asked.

He nodded to his cot across the doorway. "They won't get through me."

She pulled her knees to her chest. "Thanks for getting me these clothes. They're much nicer than the dress."

"How's your foot?" he asked.

"Better."

"Ready to sleep now?" he asked. Their day would start before first light.

"I'll try."

He moved from her cot and returned to his. He waited for her to settle, and then he shut off the light.

What was she thinking about? What would she dream about? Who had hurt her to make her question everyone around her? He could understand her fear and apprehension about the situation, but this wasn't the first time she had been cut off from her family and staying in a military base.

When she had chosen to work on the Locker, she must have known she was committing to a lifetime of looking over her shoulder.

* * *

Griffin had not left her side the entire morning. Kit wasn't accustomed to someone hovering over her, and it was unsettling. She couldn't catch her breath with him watching her.

When she went to the shower, he checked that the bathroom was empty, then waited outside the door. As she showered, Kit realized that the military had provided some essentials like shampoo and a razor, but she wouldn't have clean undergarments. Who could she ask about that? It was a small thing to worry about, but she wanted some normalcy in her life. She was a creature of habit, and her routine had been taken from her.

Kit climbed out of the shower and wrapped herself in a bleach-smelling rough white towel. Griffin was standing in the doorway to the bathroom.

"What are you doing in here?" she asked, pulling her towel tighter around her body. She had never been naked in front of a man before, and Griffin wasn't just a man. He was an incredibly handsome and virile man.

"I told you, I am looking out for you."

"I'm trying to work something out. Could you please leave?"

"What is it that you need to work out?" he asked.

She was an adult, but she couldn't discuss something this private with a stranger. "I can't talk to you about it."

He looked around. "There's no one else to talk to."

"It's a female issue."

He lifted a brow. "If you need a tampon, I'll find one."

Kit felt her face flush hot. "It's not about a…you know." A man hadn't ever talked to her like this.

"Isn't that what you mean by female issue?" he asked.

Kit liked that he was keeping his word to her and speaking simply. With him, she didn't have to read between the lines. "No." She might as well tell him. He'd solve it without making a big deal or embarrassing her. "I don't have any clean underwear, and I wasn't wearing a bra under my dress. Or socks. I'll need fresh bandages for my foot, too."

He gave her a look up and down. "I'll get what you need." He stepped out of the room for a moment and returned. "They are on their way."

Feeling better knowing she'd have more clothes between her and Griffin's perceptive eyes soon, she relaxed. She secured her towel around her, walked to the sink and combed the knots from her hair. Her sister had helped her arrange it last night. Now it was back to its normal shape, which was not much of a shape at all.

One knock on the door and Griffin opened it, standing between her and the person on the other side. He closed the door and handed her a bag. "Get dressed. The chopper leaves in five minutes." He turned around to give her privacy but stayed in the room.

Kit dressed and then sat to rewrap her foot.

"Are you finished?" he asked.

She had taken less than three minutes. Her bathroom routine was quick compared to most women's. "Just need to wrap my foot."

Griffin left his post and knelt at her feet. "Let me help you."

"How much time does it take you to get ready?" she asked. She had hurried. If he was annoyed, that was too bad.

"Minutes. Less if needed. But I'm concerned about this injury. I want to be sure it doesn't get infected." He used great care examining and bandaging her foot. Putting on socks didn't hurt. Shoes did. So did walking on it.

"I can carry you," Griffin said.

She refused to be that dependent on him. "I'll hobble." She'd figure out a way to walk to put the least amount of pressure on her foot even if it made her gait clumsy.

Griffin didn't leave her side and was patient with her slow walk. They were escorted to a field. After a few minutes, a chopper touched down close to them.

Kit moved faster, but she tripped over a divot in the grass. Before she could face-plant, Griffin grabbed her arm, keeping her upright.

"Careful. No more injuries," he said.

She had been trying to be careful. "Thank you."

Griffin supported her on the side of her injured foot, and they walked the rest of the way to the chopper.

They climbed inside. The chopper was similar to the one that had taken her to the secret military facility where she had lived for a year. For that trip, she had been blindfolded. It had been terrifying and exciting.

If she had known what that year would be like, if she had known what her work would entail and what it would mean to have a successful project, would she have done it? She had been naive and filled with self-importance. She'd thought her work would revolutionize cybersecurity. She'd believed her research would lead to malicious hackers and black hats being exposed.

The government hadn't been interested in her work being applied to any systems other than their own. They didn't care if anyone else was victimized as long as their computer systems were safe. By the time she had realized that, the project was almost complete. She had been used and cast aside, and nondisclosures and noncompete clauses prevented her from using her algorithms in other applications. Thinking of it still burned.

Griffin touched her shoulder, and heat zipped over her. He mouthed a question: "Are you okay?"

She nodded. It was too loud to talk over the spinning rotors, and Kit was glad. She didn't want to tell him she had been used then, she was being used now and in all likelihood, so was he.

Kit was driving him mad. The moment they landed, he would hand her over to the protection specialist assigned to the case and put distance between them. Connor would have had enough time to get a resource in place. Griffin was the wrong man for the job.

Griffin's entire body heated as he realized he was attracted to Kit Walker. She was part girl next door who had no idea how appealing she was and part smart professor who had a room full of male students fantasizing about sleeping with her. He was interested in her, and that awareness switched his desire on high. He wouldn't act like a sex-starved lunatic; he was a professional. But it was getting harder to keep those boundaries clear in his thoughts.

From what he'd read about her and what he had witnessed, she had a touch of social awkwardness, yet he didn't feel uncomfortable around her. He guessed she had spent so much time in her sister's shadow and then as a supergenius online, she didn't interact as naturally with people face-to-face. But when he engaged her in a topic she enjoyed, that clumsiness melted away and she was magnetic.

If she'd been more aware of her feminine prowess, she would not have stood in front of him in a towel or crammed herself next to him in this copter. He'd sat in the bathroom while she had dried herself and dressed, giving her privacy with his eyes, but his thoughts were borderline indecent. He had imagined her rubbing the towel over her soft skin, sliding her clothes on, and he had wanted to watch.

He had to keep his attraction to her in check. Maybe the leftover adrenaline from the escape the night before was still charging in his veins, but his thoughts centered on her more than the Incognito assassins they had evaded.

Her big brown eyes had been the first trait he had noticed about her. But now he enjoyed her brain and her humility. Someone in her position could be demanding and egotistical about what she had accomplished. If she realized how much the West Company and the United States government needed her, she wasn't capitalizing on it.

The pilot turned around and handed them blindfolds and earplugs. "Eyes and ears covered."

Kit did as he asked without question. She had been through this before.

She reached for Griffin's hand and slipped hers inside his. Kit was scared and she needed him. He sensed it in how she watched him and spoke to him. She was looking to him for guidance and reassurance that they were safe.

It was a heavy weight to carry, and it made him feel guilty for his thoughts of dumping her on someone else. But what could he do? Keep a job he was unqualified for? Could he handle being close to her, knowing he was attracted to her, and maintain objectivity?

Soon she would be in the care of a protection specialist, someone who hadn't let his wife die. Placing Kit with another operative with the right skills was better for everyone involved. He knew where the line was, and he wouldn't cross it with Kit.

After a short ride, the helicopter touched down. They were allowed to remove their blindfolds and earplugs. They would be met by one of the West Company's operatives. Griffin would complete the hand-off, go to his debriefing and then return home and wait for his next assignment.

Done and done.

Kit didn't release him. He was helping her with her injury, but her hand gripped his clothing as if she was afraid they would be separated.

"I'm here," he whispered to her.

"I hate not knowing where we are," she said.

"We're safe. That's priority one," Griffin said. He couldn't get to his gun as easily with her hand in his. Her hands were shaking, giving away she was nervous.

In a small, comfortable room with plush tan carpeting and beige furniture, they were offered drinks. Trays of fruit, cheese, small sandwiches and vegetables were set in the middle of the table. The pictures on the wall were of generic floral arrangements.

A man Griffin didn't recognize entered the room. "Thank you for your help in this matter. You may consider your service complete. Mr. Brooks, please come with me."

"Wait," Kit said. "You're leaving me?" She sounded shocked, and her voice quavered.

"You'll be working with someone more skilled to handle your unique situation," Griffin said. He heard the words and hated how bureaucratic he sounded. He wasn't the right man for the job, and knowing it stung. He had reached the end of the line for him and Kit. Kit was safest with someone who could protect her without thinking of her naked and writhing on his sheets.

"My unique situation? What is unique about my situation?" She didn't hide her anger.

Griffin didn't want to talk about this in front of a stranger. "Your skills are needed."

She narrowed her gaze at Griffin. "If you walk away from me, I swear I will be less than useless. I know what you want me to do, and I am exclusively skilled to help you in this matter. But my memory might suddenly take a nosedive, and perhaps I'll forget everything."

The other man looked between them. "Is there something about your relationship with the target that we're unaware of?" He addressed the question to Griffin. Griffin heard the accusation in the words.

"No," Griffin said at the same time Kit said, "Yes."

How should he respond to this situation? Laugh it off? Try to explain about Kit? Reassure her she was safer with someone else?

She was scared. She needed to feel safe. Everyone did. "Kit, I was sent to retrieve you and bring you in. I've done that."

"You said you would stay until you knew I was safe," she said.

"I know you are safe," Griffin said, hoping he sounded confident.

"I don't feel safe. I don't know anyone here," Kit said.

She was digging in her heels, creating an impasse.

"I'll get Connor," the man said and left the room.

"Kit," Griffin said, trying to reason with her now that they were alone. "You'll lead everyone to believe I've done something wrong."

Kit stared at him. "Wrong? I'm still alive. That means you've done something very right. I feel safe with you. I don't want to be passed around."

Connor West entered the room. Griffin stood to attention, even though this wasn't a military op. The man had that presence. He commanded and got respect. All the operatives who worked for him felt better with him at their backs. Griffin knew he had likely gotten little sleep, but Connor was clean shaven, his clothes pressed and his close-cropped brown hair tidy.

"Kit Walker, it is a pleasure to meet you. I'm Connor West," he said. Connor's voice was warm and genuine.

Connor didn't shake her hand. Her profile had indicated she didn't like intrusions on her personal space.

Kit glared at Griffin. "I'm not changing my mind no matter whom you parade in here."

Connor didn't appear upset by her hostile tone, but rather amused. "You want Griffin to stay with you. Could you tell me why?"

Kit looked at Griffin. "He's killed to protect me. I can trust him."

Connor nodded his agreement. "I like having Griffin on the team. I trust him implicitly."

"Connor, can we speak in private?" Connor wouldn't force Griffin to take up the post as Kit's protector, but Griffin felt the question coming. Should he tell Connor the whole truth about how he felt about Kit? His attraction to her could deepen, and the deeper the attraction, the more dangerous the situation.

Kit folded her arms and sat. "Go ahead."

He and Connor walked into the hallway. "What is the nature of her feelings for you?" Connor asked.

"She's been through a lot. She's attached to me. You know her profile. She's guarded."

"We need her. We need her calm and in control," Connor said. "The safety and security of the United States government depend on it."

Griffin rubbed his temples, where a headache was forming. Aside from his concerns about his ability to maintain professionalism with her, he had other problems that needed to be addressed—like, say, his track record showing he couldn't keep someone safe. "She says she'll make herself useless if I leave her."

"Tell me what I can do to make this work," Connor said. "You know her better than I do."

"She's smart. She may feign ignorance about the project, especially if she's scared." If she bowed out of helping them, they wouldn't have a way to safeguard the Locker or counter Incognito's threats.

"We need to convince her to help, and she may be more willing to help if she remains with you. Can you do that?" Connor asked.

"I am not trained to be someone's bodyguard. That's not my area of expertise."

"You can handle this," Connor said.

It was on the tip of his tongue to tell Connor about his attraction to Kit. But Griffin could keep it in check. He wasn't a slave to his hormones. Too much was at stake for him to give in to his feelings. Instead, he made the point that mattered most. "My wife died because I couldn't protect her. What makes you think I can keep Kit safe?"

"This situation is nothing like what happened with Beth. No one blames you for Beth's death except you. What could you have done differently?"

At the mention of his wife's name, disgust for himself and anger at her killer renewed. "I ask myself that every day."

"The answer eludes you because there is no answer. You couldn't have done anything. What happened with Beth was a terrible atrocity, but protecting Kit will be different. You will be at her side around the clock. She is your sole mission."

Griffin didn't care for his body's response to hearing that. As a red-blooded man, he wanted to be close to Kit. As an operative, he was inadequate to protect her.

Kit and Griffin were given accommodations, nicer ones than they'd had at the military base. Kit had even been issued a rolling suitcase filled with clothing and essentials. The clothes were in her size. Creepy, but Kit had been thoroughly investigated before becoming part of the Locker team, and she wasn't surprised to learn every detail of her life had been recorded.

"We need to go on the offensive," Griffin said.

"On the offensive against Incognito?" Kit asked.

"Yes. Covertly. You can strike back."

"At Incognito?" she repeated. It sounded insane.

She wasn't a hacker who enjoyed hurting people, and she liked to avoid trouble. Obtaining her security clearance to be part of the Locker team had required an aversion to creating problems. While some people thrived off drama, Kit liked her life to be trouble-free.

"This will play out one of two ways. They will win or we will. Incognito will continue coming after you and everyone on the team until we stop them," he said.

"You and me against Incognito?" she asked.

He shook his head. "Don't think in those terms. We have the West Company behind us."

"Except Incognito managed to find me," Kit said.

"This is a challenge you'll enjoy."

A thrill traced through her at the idea of getting back into the game against a real competitor. "I didn't work on the Locker alone. I need people with very specific skill sets."

"Tell me where to find them."

She took great joy in speaking her next words. "Gamer Con."

"The video game convention?" Griffin asked.

She had attended whenever possible, three times in the past decade. She'd loved it every time. "Yes, a video game convention. Thousands of the world's biggest computer and gaming enthusiasts packed into one conference center. The place will be humming with talent."

Griffin ran a hand through his hair. He seemed resigned, but not excited. "Tell me how to get tickets and I'll clear it with Connor."

* * *

The flight from their meeting with Connor West to Las Vegas, Nevada took less than an hour. It took three times that to make the security arrangements and convince Connor West that Kit's plan was safe and would have a positive outcome.

Gamer Con was the world's biggest video game enthusiast convention. Kit hadn't attended in a number of years, but she had a few online friends skilled at hacking who would be there.

The easiest part about Gamer Con for Griffin and Kit's cover was the ability to blend. Gamers wore jeans and T-shirts as well as costumes of favorite video game characters. Incognito had been targeting events like Gamer Con looking for members of the Locker project. Griffin was on high alert.

"Have you ever played a video game?" Kit asked Griffin as he parked his car in the multilevel garage behind the hotel.

"I have," he said.

"Recently?"

"Not recently. A shooting game isn't as fun when I've been involved in the real thing. When I'm not working, I don't like to handle a gun or pretend I'm handling a gun."

"Not all video games are violent and involve guns," Kit said, though most of the ones she played did have elements of fighting, even if it was with fantasy weapons.

"If we need to play games here, I can hold my own. Don't worry about me."

She wasn't worried about him. Everything she had seen about Griffin spoke to how competent and capable he was. "I ordered costumes from a local boutique and paid the rush fee for them to arrive today. They should be waiting for us at the front desk."

"Costumes?" Griffin asked. "What's wrong with what we're wearing?"

"To hide from Incognito, we can dress as our favorite video game characters," she said.

"I don't have a favorite video game character," he said.

"My favorite video characters," she clarified.

"I'm not wearing a tutu," he said.

She smirked at the idea of him in a pink tutu, the pure ludicrousness of his six-foot-something muscled self crammed into a delicate tulle skirt. "I would never be so cruel to you."

A woman and man with their faces painted green and wearing purple latex jumpsuits walked by.

"Oh. Okay. I got it," Griffin said. "Who will we dress as? Want to give me a clue?"

She wouldn't ruin the surprise or give him a chance to protest. "You'll see." Seeing Griffin dressed as a video game hero held an enormous appeal. He could rock the buff bad boy look better than most of the men she knew. He had that even without the costume.

They slipped on their sunglasses. Anyone recognizing her was unlikely, and while she was at Gamer

Con, she would use only her most recent online alias,
Orchid. Lotus was dead, and if Kit wanted to survive
this, it needed to stay that way.

Chapter 4

"Stay close to me," Griffin said.

The conference center was crowded. Without the West Company, it was unlikely they would have been able to book a room in the connected hotel. Though the temperature outside was in the nineties and humid, the hotel was a frosty sixty degrees. A pianist at the baby grand in the lobby played classical renditions of video game tunes.

"Griffin?" she asked.

He stopped and turned to her. "What?"

"You're walking like a Fed."

"A Fed? You mean like a federal agent?"

"Yes," she said. "You need to walk more casually. This conference attracts tons of hackers from around the world. Because of that, federal agents come here to recruit hackers or to look for wanted ones. You don't want to be pegged as a Fed."

Griffin stared at her. "What happens if I'm pegged as a Fed?"

"People will avoid you. Because I'm with you, they might think I'm one, only better at keeping my cover, and therefore be unwilling to talk to me."

He relaxed his shoulders and slowed his gait. The change was remarkable. When he wasn't rushing, his slow, easy mannerisms indicated he was relaxed. She guessed he rarely relaxed, and not while working.

They entered the hotel, and a couple darted between them.

Her social anxiety ticked up. Many people stuffed in a small space. Kit slipped her hand into his. "I don't want to lose you."

Griffin's hand was firm and strong. If the conference became too crazy, she would close her eyes and let him lead her.

They checked into their room, and Griffin handed her a keycard. The front desk slid Griffin a large box that was waiting under their aliases.

Griffin looked at the box and then at her. "How elaborate are these costumes?"

Fairly elaborate. The costumes would conceal her identity. The wig and sunglasses she was wearing could only do so much.

"We'll fit in," she said.

Griffin glanced at a couple walking by in matching bright yellow jumpsuits. He said nothing to her, but she saw the brief flash of amusement pull up the corners of his mouth.

Griffin gathered their box, and Kit pulled their suitcases.

"We're on the fiftieth floor. I don't like being that high," Griffin said.

"Scared of heights?" she asked.

He snorted. "I've jumped from airplanes. It's not the height that's a problem. Fiftieth floor is high enough that we can't jump to safety."

Was he always thinking about the next attack? She was the same way when she was designing software. Every line of code, every call to a database had to be checked and rechecked for flaws. That attention to detail was what had made the Locker so valuable and impenetrable. She and the team had tried to exploit each other's work, and every single breach had been closed.

They took the elevator to their room. After three floors, the elevator stopped, and a trio stepped in. The man in the middle had a woman on either side of him. Both women were dressed in short, provocative dresses. One had her hand down the front of the man's pants, and the other stroked his chest.

The woman closest to them looked at Griffin and licked her lips. "Room forty forty-three if you're interested in joining us."

Griffin smiled. "Thanks. That's a nice offer."

Kit couldn't see his eyes behind his sunglasses, but he was lying. The threesome exited the elevator and they were again alone.

When the doors closed, Kit set her hands on Griffin and mimicked the woman who'd been stroking the other man's bare, hairy chest. "Room forty forty-three is your next stop?"

Griffin stilled her hands. "No, but keep that up and the bed will be."

Because of a playful touch? She had been kidding around, but he sounded mad. Was he frustrated she had trapped him into this assignment with her? Kit went silent and pressed her hands to her sides. If he didn't want to be touched, she would respect that. She despised introductory handshakes and hugs, and she understood everyone had boundaries.

When they arrived in their room, she frowned. One small room, two double beds. No privacy. "Can't we get a suite? Or connecting rooms?"

"I need to watch you. I'll give you as much space as I can while keeping you safe."

Griffin set the box he'd been carrying under his arm on the floor. Kit clapped her hands. Her costumes! She couldn't wait to try them.

She ripped at the packing tape sealing the box shut, but it was hard to open. Griffin pulled a knife, wordlessly moved her hands aside and sliced through the tape.

His first outfit was on top. Faux leather jacket, tight black T-shirt, black jeans and black sunglasses. She held up the pieces to show him. "Do you like it?"

He eyed it. "What is it? I mean, what character does it belong to?"

"Don't worry. Not a woman or anything. You're

a vampire. More specifically, a dark lord of the fifth realm."

He arched a brow. "Will there be a quiz?"

She shook her head. If anyone asked him about the game, she could cover for him.

"What about you?" he asked. "Leather, too?"

She shook her head and drew hers out of the box. "You'll see." She scampered into the bathroom to try it on. The dress was short, coming about six inches above her knee. The top was as she'd pictured it, high neck and long sleeves. When she was dressed, she opened the door to the bathroom.

Griffin had changed into his costume. Though she'd wanted a reaction from him, her reaction was summed up in a few words: sexy, drop-dead gorgeous god. Griffin was an attractive man. His face was unabashedly masculine with a straight nose and strong jawline. His full lips looked utterly kissable. He looked like he had stepped off the screen of the video game "Dark Rising." He had the muscles and the tone and the build. Broad shoulders tapered to a trim waist and long legs.

"You look great," she said, the words coming at a stammer. Their costumes were supposed to help them blend. Griffin would draw attention, at least from the women. He would play a starring role in every woman's fantasy.

Griffin's gaze wandered up and down her body, stopping at her legs. "Are we a couple?"

She wished. Like on her best day she could be the girlfriend of a man like Griffin. She wouldn't know how to handle him and a relationship that involved face-to-face contact and time together in bed. Did their cover at Gamer Con include pretending they were lovers? They were sharing a room. "In the game, your character protects mine. We have an on-again, off-again relationship. It's touch and go. We are lovers and fighters."

Griffin blinked at her. "There's sex in video games?"

Sex crept in, especially in role-playing games. "Staying home on a weekend night to play means a slim possibility of getting laid. Tensions are played out on the screen."

"I wouldn't have guessed," Griffin said, rubbing his chin.

This conversation was making her skin tingle and ache to be touched. Talking about the video game was easy for her, but she didn't know how to make the discussion of sex cross into real life. Could she tell Griffin she found him attractive, especially dressed as he was? "Are you ready to hit the conference? I have a list of people I want to track down."

Griffin nodded toward the door. "Lead the way. I'm at your back."

His pants were too tight, and his erection was straining to pop out of them. Kit seemed excited about the characters and playing dress-up like it was Halloween, but his body cared only about how good Kit looked in her dress. If he was supposed to be a vampire and she wanted him to stick to his role, he could suck her neck or somewhere she found pleasing.

Knowing the thought was inappropriate and shaking it off, he followed Kit into the elevator. His costume gave him places to hide his weapons. His character was a gun-carrying vampire. Griffin's were real, but if anyone asked, he would play them off as props.

Griffin slid his arm over her shoulders. She grinned up at him. "In the video game, your character leads mine around by a collar."

Griffin jolted. "What?" He would slip into this role, but dragging her around by the throat was beyond anything he was comfortable doing.

She laughed. "I'm joking. But you might see stuff like that here. Don't act shocked. If you were a gamer, then it would be nothing to you."

Being with Kit, it was hard to ignore the energy and excitement in the air and easy to get caught in the drama.

"Stay close." He needed to protect her, and she might need to translate or cover for him if they were pulled into a video game conversation.

They paid their entrance fee and entered a huge conference room with rows of vendors selling game products and accessories, new games, comic books, high-tech equipment, energy drinks and bars and an assortment of fan memorabilia.

Most notable were the conference attendees. His and Kit's outfits fit in with those of the gamers, though Kit's costume was the most sensual. Not nearly bare breasts and skirt to the ass dimple, but

showing enough skin to entice him and leaving something to the imagination.

Griffin ignored the looks she was receiving from
other gamers. He didn't believe that anyone recognized her as Lotus, one of the world's most famous
hackers. He interpreted the looks as interest—in getting her to their rooms. Wouldn't happen. Kit stayed
with him, and he would watch over her.

Did Kit notice their glances? Maybe when she was
with her sister the supermodel, she was accustomed
to being ignored, but here, away from her sister's
shadow, it was easy for Kit to grab attention.

Kit turned and pressed her face against him. His
left arm instinctively went around her, and his right
reached for his gun.

He pulled her out of the center of the walkway.
"Tell me," he said.

"I see someone I shouldn't recognize, but I do." She
looked up at him with the most doe-eyed expression
he'd seen in years. How was this innocent-looking
woman responsible for a superamped cybersecurity
system protecting the United States' most critical
data?

"Tell me who he is," Griffin said.

"Rezwald. He's a hacker for hire. He was brought
in to break into the Locker during testing. He couldn't
do it while working as a contractor. Once his contract ended, he tried to break in again. For fun. He
almost succeeded."

"You think he's helping Incognito now?"

"Maybe. Depends how much information Incognito has on the project. Rezwald was a black box tester. Rez didn't have access to the code or the hardware it ran on, but he had access to the console to break in."

"You think he broke into the Locker and discovered something?" Griffin asked. Information like that would be valuable to Incognito.

She didn't move away from him. "Maybe."

"Would he recognize you?" he asked.

She appeared uncertain. "Hackers knew Lotus was working on the Locker. But my face wasn't attached to my old alias, and for the past several years, I've been Orchid. I also don't post my picture with that name. I recognize him because I made knowing everything I could about the Locker my business. If I discovered his identity, he could have discovered mine."

"We won't take chances. I'll alert Connor that he's here and ask him to send someone to keep an eye on him. Let me know if you recognize anyone else related to the project."

Griffin sent the information to Connor. As they walked through the booths, Kit seemed tense. He didn't blame her. While this place was ripe with people they could use for their team, it was also thick with wanted criminals and threats to their safety.

Kit's breasts were rubbing against the vampire costume. It was a little tight through the bust, which provided good support, but it was also making her aware of her desire for Griffin. The hem of her skirt brushing against her thighs added to the effect. Feeling feminine and sexy in Griffin's presence was a dangerous thing.

He was experienced with women. He knew how to seduce a woman. Without a keyboard in front of her, Kit was lost.

Seeing Rezwald had shaken her. He could know who she was. After all, she knew his face even though she wasn't supposed to. She had been assured that no one would know she had worked on the Locker, yet her identity had been uncovered by Incognito. Who else knew Kit Walker was Lotus?

As they passed one of the vendors, a man shoved a small black ticket into her hands. "You look like a couple who enjoys having fun."

The man eyed her and Griffin with equal interest. Glancing at the ticket, Kit almost handed it back to him. She wasn't interested in Ménage-Play, a rave held every year during Gamer Con, but off the premises. It wasn't an official event sanctioned by the conference. Too many incidents in years past made Gamer Con distance itself from Ménage-Play: drugs, drinking to excess, sex acts on the dance floor, fights and police involvement.

Griffin took the ticket and nodded his thanks.

"What's this?" he asked as they wandered away. "Ménage-Play?"

"A rave," she said. "I haven't attended, but according to rumors, it's a party with music pulled from video games and remixed. Very intense." Lots of half-naked people gyrating and grinding on each other and looking to play out fantasies they'd had while gaming.

"Will any of the people you want to speak with be there?" Griffin asked.

"Maybe." She had some gamer friends who talked about the yearly rave like it was the mecca for sex.

"Then we'll go."

Kit shook her head. "It's not my scene." Being touched by strangers made her uncomfortable. Actually, that wasn't the right word. Being touched by strangers *panicked* her.

"What are you afraid will happen?" Griffin asked.

"Lots of stuff could happen," she said. She lowered her voice. "People have sex in the open in front of other people. That's not my thing. And the drinking and the drugs are crazy. If any of my friends are there, they wouldn't be in a state to talk about a serious matter."

"Under the influence, people will let their guards down," Griffin said.

Even so, screaming over music and being mashed against sweaty, oversexed people wasn't her idea of fun.

"We wouldn't have to partake in any of the substances," he said.

"If you want to go, then go. I'll stay in our hotel room." She was offering because he wouldn't leave her. Let Connor West send someone else to Ménage-Play if he wanted to know more about it.

"We're staying together. We're going to this rave."

Kit frowned. "Why do you want me to go so badly?"

"We have limited time to find the people you're

looking for. You admitted they might be there. We have to take every opportunity."

She couldn't imagine herself at a rave. "Did you see me at my sister's birthday party?" Which had been a million times tamer, at least until Griffin and the Incognito gunmen had arrived.

"I saw you."

"If you saw me, you know I don't socialize well. I was uncomfortable. How will I feel at a rave?"

Griffin put his arm around her. "I'll be with you. I won't leave you all night."

Kit sighed. He looked at her in a way that made it impossible to say no. Nothing about this or the Locker had been easy for her. They could attend and leave if she couldn't handle it. "Guess we're going to a rave."

Ménage-Play was as crowded and hot and insane as Kit had imagined. The party was taking place in a rehabbed warehouse downtown, about two blocks from the hotel. The area was divided into three spaces, each blaring music and a thump that hurt her head. A hallway extended away from the main rooms. Kit assumed the hallway was lined with rooms for those looking for an intimate, but private, experience.

Griffin was pressed behind Kit, and a young blonde woman wearing a silver bikini was grinding into her. She had hair to her waist, and it curled at the ends like ocean waves.

Kit tried to move away. In the crowd, it took a full minute to shuffle three inches. The woman giggled when Kit was out of the way. Silver Bikini reached for Griffin and pressed her hips against his, leaving no question what she had in mind. It was the same thought every woman had when she saw Griffin. He looked incredible tonight, still wearing part of his vampire costume, the tight black T-shirt and dark jeans. He had removed the leather jacket and sunglasses, but the outfit worked on him.

Kit had known this would happen. She had no interest in standing by while women ground their half-naked bodies against Griffin. It was hard for him to blend. He was a head taller than most of the men and broader across the shoulders.

Should she put more distance between them? Should she tell Griffin it was okay if he wanted to leave with one of the women eyeing him?

To her surprise, Griffin pivoted away from Silver Bikini and instead put Kit in front of him. He didn't even look at the other woman with longing. Shock rippled over her and following on its heels was a jolt of happiness. Griffin had picked her.

The music volume made conversation impossible. The rhythmic thumping vibrated her. Someone passed by her, brushing against her, a hand lingering on her leg. She wished she had changed from her vampire outfit into pants that covered more of her.

She wanted to go home. Kit moved toward the door. Griffin grabbed her hand and asked her something, but she couldn't hear him over the music. He brought his mouth close to her ear, but even then, she made out only disjointed syllables.

Griffin turned her to face him. He positioned his

big body around her and she instantly felt safe as
if sectioned off from the crowd. In the circle of his
arms, no one else touched her. Griffin ignored the
women who pounded against him with their curvy
hips and big beach-ball breasts. His eyes were on her
and only her.

He was forgoing sex to watch over her. She was
the focus of his absolute attention. Her skin tingled
with awareness, and desire enveloped her. Was she
misreading him, or was he into her? This was one
area of her life where she had little experience. If she
could have called Marissa, she would have. Marissa
would know. When it came to men, Kit didn't trust
her own instincts.

After almost wrestling her hormones under control, the song changed, and Griffin put his hands on
her shoulders. For a man who seemed uptight much
of the time, he could dance. His fluid motion, as if
the music were part of him, had her moving with
him. She closed her eyes and followed the rhythm
of his body.

As they danced, Kit pretended she was the video
game character Liliana Sole, vampire and soul collec-
tor, and Griffin was Clash, her lover, her soul mate,
the man she was meant to be with forever and who
would protect her until the end of time.

What would that feel like? To have a man like
Griffin infatuated with her? *Infatuation* had a nega-
tive connotation, but if it was in a reciprocal, must-
have-each-other way, couldn't that work? Her sister
had a long series of relationships with men who were

obsessed with her. They'd profess their love; they'd shower her with gifts, attention and affection. They would watch her move through a crowd as if she were the single most fascinating creature in existence.

Kit had been jealous of that attention and had wished for a man to look at her that way. Griffin was watching her, perhaps not with lust and longing, but with something akin to desire, and she felt powerful.

Her sister's relationships didn't last. They burned too quick and too hot and flamed themselves out. The key to a happy relationship might have been finding that sizzling, spicy love and building a foundation under it.

Kit wanted a man to send her flowers, take her to dinner and buy her a drink, dating rituals she had heard of but hadn't experienced. Her skin felt flushed, and her palms itched to reach for Griffin. This might be the only chance she had to touch a man who looked like him. He couldn't—wouldn't—run away, and while the possibility of rejection was high, she could claim she had lost herself in the music.

She rubbed against him harder, lust humming in her veins. She squeezed his biceps, feeling the roped muscle beneath the tight skin. Leaning forward, she brushed her chest against his, her nipples feeling sensitive to the point of pain.

Griffin had his hand on her lower back, and the state of his erection left no question that he was turned on. By her? By the experience?

A woman in a red devil costume extended her hand to Griffin, a purple pill in her palm. Some designer drug, likely used to heighten sensation. Griffin shook his head, as Kit knew he would. The woman shrugged, smiled and popped the pill in her mouth. Kit had never taken illegal drugs. She was too afraid of what they would do to her or what she would do under the influence.

Griffin put space between them, and she felt the loss of the connection in her gut. She was jolted out of her fantasy realm and fell hard into reality. She was a nerd being used by the government, again, for her computer skills and her connections. Griffin had been coerced, by duty or guilt or maybe the promise of a big payday, to look out for her. Believing his motives lay anywhere else was deluding herself.

Kit gestured to the door and made a sign of pleading. She couldn't talk to anyone this way, and she wanted to leave. She was overheated. She wanted a drink and didn't trust anything the bar served.

Now that a series of depressing emotions caught up to her, she wanted a lemon-lime soda and a box of icing-stuffed chocolate cookies. That would make her feel better. Emotional eating, but it was sugar binge or demand Griffin take her to a sex toy shop so she could find a vibrator to take the edge off. It was the only bedroom activity she was proficient at, and she needed release.

Whatever Griffin had done to her desire, it was worked into a frenzy, and she needed to sate it.

Griffin nodded. The room was crowded, but as he moved, people made way for him.

Once outside the building, they had a two-block

walk to their hotel. The sidewalks and streets were busy despite the late hour, and the lights from the hotel illuminated the area.

Griffin touched his hips, where he had his guns and knife. "You okay?"

"That isn't my scene," she said.

"I thought we would run into someone important."

She shook her head. "I can't think with so much noise and so many people. I couldn't focus on who was there with people touching me." Her skin tingled, and she felt a wave of dizziness.

"I tried to keep them off you."

Being close to Griffin had worked her up in a different way. "The issue was keeping women off you."

He inclined his head. "I don't care if people bump into me."

He was a rock. Of course he wouldn't. Had he missed the intention in those women's eyes? "I don't think those women were just bumping into you. They were propositioning you."

Griffin made a sound of acknowledgment. "Wasn't my first rave. It's not my scene, either."

Hadn't he enjoyed the attention of the women who had surrounded him? "You could have chosen one of those women to take home." Why was she picking at this wound? What did she want him to say? That he would love to have taken home one or two women to see what fun they could have?

"Maybe I could have. I wouldn't."

She should have let the conversation drop. "Because you're working."

"I'm working, and I was there with you."

Loyalty. Interesting. "I could have fended for myself."

"Undoubtedly. But I didn't want some man groping you. The only way to stop that was to make it clear to every person who came within a foot of you that you were mine. *Are* mine."

His possessiveness struck a chord with her, and she felt as if the air had been sucked from her lungs. Her skin prickled and her insides clutched with yearning. "Do you feel strange?"

Concern crossed his face. "No, do you? What do you need?"

She was tingling across her breasts and between her legs, like an itch demanding she scratch it, stroke it, handle it. "Sex." And a soda. Cookies. Mostly sex, though.

Griffin drew himself to full height. "I can't help you with that, and I won't approve of you picking a partner to take to our hotel room. Not until I've screened him, and that will take days."

"No sex, then?" she asked, her breasts feeling heavy.

"No sex."

As they walked, an ache, a deep throb between her legs, pulsed distractingly. A chill swept over her from her head to her feet, leaving her core feeling hot and the rest of her exposed. "Griffin, I feel sick."

Griffin faced her. "Did you eat anything in that club? Drink anything?"

She shook her head. "You were with me the entire time."

Griffin lifted her and carried her beneath the streetlight. He searched her, kneeling in front of her and running his hands over her bare skin.

"That's not helping me not want sex," she said, pressing into his hands as they moved over her. His touch was so good. Too good.

He swore and pulled something from her thigh. It stung like ripping off an adhesive bandage.

"What is that?" she asked.

He took out his phone, snapped a picture of it and slipped it into his pocket. "You were drugged."

Her eyes went wide. "With what?" She hadn't taken anything stronger than over-the-counter medicine in her life.

"It explains why you've been talking to me so frankly. And why you're rubbing against me."

She was not aware she had been. She stilled her body.

Griffin lifted her and raced with her in his arms toward their hotel room.

Chapter 5

Carrying Kit through the hotel while she was moaning—a low moan, like she was in the throes of passion—invited stares. Since they were trying to stay under the radar, Griffin tucked her head against his shoulder to prevent anyone from recognizing her. His phone was vibrating, but he couldn't answer it.

Every movement elicited more moans from her. She licked his neck. If he hadn't had a tight grip on her, he would have dropped her. The elevator came quickly, and once inside, they were mercifully alone. As they reached their room, he set Kit down to fish out his key card. She slid her hand into his pocket. He caught her wrist and stopped her.

"I know you feel different right now, but give me a few minutes." He opened the door to their hotel room and hustled her inside. "I need to call Connor and find out what we need to do."

Kit sat on the maroon chair by the window. She was moaning and touching herself, running her hands over her breasts and between her legs. Distracting, but Griffin could handle it.

His phone beeped, and he had his answers for why and what was happening to her. The drug she'd been given was absorbed through the skin. It was a designer drug with the street name "rapture." It made the user feel a flood of serotonin and crave sex.

"Griffin, come here and talk to me." She had lifted her leg high on the chair, her short skirt sliding to her hip.

Not a chance. Holding her and having her crawl all over him was a mistake. He called Connor immediately. "Tell me the cure."

"No cure. It has to work its way out of her system. Put her in the shower. Get the rest off her skin. Give her water and flush it out. That's the only advice I have for now. I'm making more calls to find out if we can do anything else. If it's too unbearable, I can get a doctor to you to drug her, maybe with morphine or alprazolam, but I don't know how the drugs interact and what's safe for her."

He wouldn't describe what she was doing now, but it was turning him on, and he was ashamed of that. He was supposed to protect her. That meant no sex, especially no sex when she wasn't in her right mind.

"Griffin, I ache," she said, peeling off her top.

She was wearing a red lace bra underneath. A test

of his control. He was a good man, and no matter what she said, he would not give in to her.

"Can I let her take care of it herself?" Griffin asked. Would that make her feel better? Watching her suffer was hard.

Connor cleared his throat. "I can't see the harm in that. Don't leave her alone, though. Watch her."

A drugged-up Kit who demanded sex, and he could only watch. Griffin had been trained to withstand torture and have absolute control of his body. He could get through this without touching her inappropriately. He could hide his thoughts. She didn't need to know he was attracted to her. He thanked Connor and disconnected.

"We need to get you in the shower," he said.

Kit giggled. "You want us to take a shower?"

"Solo. I'll help you if you need it," he said, feeling at a loss for words. Putting off a woman he was drawn to wasn't easy.

She ran her hands over her bra. "I need you to touch me."

"That's the drug talking," he said.

She slung her feet to the floor and crossed the room to him, moving stealthily. She grabbed the hem of his shirt and lifted it.

He removed her hands. "Stop."

She pouted. "Don't be a spoilsport. I bet you've done this plenty of times."

"Taken advantage of a woman under the influence? No, never." He preferred his encounters with women to be sober.

"You wouldn't be taking advantage of me. I'm giving you the advantage."

She was coming on to him, and resisting made his brain feel like it would explode.

Kit reached for his belt buckle. He again stilled her hands. He walked backward to the bathroom. "You need to get in the shower and rinse your skin. You'll feel better after that." He hoped. He could please a woman in the way Kit needed right now, but he was not sure how to do that without touching her.

She ran her fingers through his hair and pulled it a little. She tried to kiss him, and he turned his head. She dropped to her knees and ran her hand down the front of his pants.

"Kit, stand up." His voice was harsh, but he felt his control slipping. "Shower. Now. We have to make sure your skin is clear."

She frowned. He stalked into the bathroom.

She followed him inside and began removing her clothes. He looked away and counted, said the alphabet, boring recitations that wouldn't make him think of her and climbing in that shower with her.

Anything she said was the drug talking. She did not want this.

"You are so uptight," she said, standing behind him, resting her head on his back and reaching around him.

"Why are your abs this way?" She was moving her hands over them.

He wasn't talking to her about his body, her body or anything their bodies could do together. "You'll feel better after a shower." That was his mantra for the night. Maybe he could run a bath. Didn't women like that? Was that a good distraction?

"Help me with my bandage?" She extended her foot.

As carefully as he could and holding her calf in his hand, Griffin removed the bandage on her foot. He ignored the sounds she was making in her throat as he touched her leg. He set her foot on the floor and stood.

Reaching into the shower, he twisted the faucet and lifted the knob for the shower. The water spurted on, cold at first and then growing hotter. As steam rose from the tub, he gestured to it. "Get in," he said. Hand on the Bible, he was doing everything he could not to look at her naked. Not to stare at her chest and her toned legs and her flat stomach. But he was a man, and despite his efforts to feel nothing while on the job, she was working every last angle and his libido was responding.

She shook her head. "Only if you will."

He wasn't beyond throwing her into the water, but he wanted to clean her body, especially where he'd found the drug strip.

He kicked off his shoes and stepped into the shower fully clothed. She followed and laughed. "You aren't any fun."

This wasn't about fun. "You need to be soaped," he said, tearing the wrapping off the hotel soap. He rubbed it over her thigh where he had found the drug. Then he soaped a washcloth and handed it to her.

"You want me clean because I'm dirty?" she asked.

She leaned forward, bracing her hands on the wall of the shower and wiggling her bottom at him.

Griffin thought of war. Of grenades. Of being in a foxhole with men who had not showered in days.

"Aren't you going to clean the rest of me?" she asked.

He wasn't. He had only cleaned the area where he'd found the drug strip because he wanted as little of it in her system as possible. Her current mood was sex and impertinence, and he wanted the job done right. "You're feeling the effects of the drug. But I need you to think. This is not who you are. This will pass. When it does, you would be furious and feel understandably violated if I did anything to you."

Why was he trying to reason with her? He wouldn't let her do something she would regret. But he needed her to tone it down.

She lifted the small bottle of shampoo and dumped some in her hair. "Please wash it."

Was this necessary? The drug wasn't in her hair. She moved closer to him. The steam from the shower and the wetness of his clothes made him uncomfortable. Uncomfortable was good now. To keep her from touching him, he spun her so the water hit her thigh. Then he washed her hair.

He hadn't washed a woman's hair before. He assumed the principles were the same as for a man's hair. She moaned and swayed under the water.

"Are you dizzy?" he asked.

"No, just really, really excited," she said.

Her backside brushed the front of his jeans. He ignored his body's involuntary response. When he was finished lathering the shampoo through her hair, he removed his hands.

"Rinse," he said.

She ducked under the spray, and soapy water filled the floor of the tub. Giggling, she reached for the handheld shower sprayer. "Look, it can do a lot of things. Clean me and help me."

She brought it between her legs and moaned. He pivoted away, feeling simultaneously responsible and guilty for watching. Moving the shower head up and down, she let out a frustrated growl. "So close, but it's not working. Please, Griffin. Help me. I know you can finish this."

No, he couldn't. He wouldn't. "Kit, you might hate me now for saying no, but you'll be happier in the morning." *Please let this wear off by morning.*

"Just pretend for twenty seconds that you're not my bodyguard. Pretend you're my lover. I'll be fast. I'm almost there."

This must have been a punishment for the times he had met a woman, slept with her and hadn't called the next day. Or retribution for some terrible crime committed in a past life. "No."

Frustration was plain on her face. She hooked the water sprayer back on the wall and reached between her legs. She propped one foot on the tub brazenly, one hand on the wall. "It's eighty percent a mental game."

"Overcoming the drug?" he asked, hoping she was

fighting it, and would collapse from exhaustion and sleep it off.

"Having an orgasm. At this moment, I am directing my energy into a fantasy I've been having since seeing you in that vampire outfit. The outfit I picked for you. Did you know it was my personal fantasy to be that character's lover?"

She let her head fall back and closed her eyes. Griffin closed his. He wasn't sure how much of this he could stand. His arousal was pressing at the zipper of his jeans insistently. At least if he couldn't see her, he could imagine something unsexy, like sweaty gym clothes and kids' used diapers. But even with his eyes closed and trying to fixate on unattractive things, he saw her. She was in front of him and his muscles twitched with awareness of it.

"I'm thinking of your hands on me. On my breasts and between my thighs. Your hands are big and they make me feel safe. Now your mouth is pressed to mine. You're a good kisser. Talented. You kiss my neck and everywhere and then you get between my legs. I spread myself open for you and then you lick me."

She shivered and cried out. Griffin opened his eyes, worried what had happened. As an orgasm ripped through her, she sat on the floor of the tub, leaning her head against the tile.

"Better. I feel better." She was panting.

He didn't feel better. His lust was overwhelming, and he felt like it was strangling him. "Let's get you dry."

"Are you worried that I'm so wet?" she asked and looked up at him with those expressive eyes.

He didn't reply to that. He couldn't. His mouth was sand and his entire focus was on keeping her safe, including from herself and him.

He stepped out of the tub and tossed her two towels from the rack. "Get dry."

"Help me," she said.

He sensed the orgasm had only taken the edge off her lust. She wanted more. "No." He was wet and now cold, but undressing wasn't an option. He needed his clothes to stay in place. Besides, it wasn't the first time he'd worn soaking wet clothes. At least their hotel room was warm.

He was a trained operative. He could withstand anything.

"These pajamas are really soft," Kit said. She pulled the bottoms on, and Griffin was grateful.

"Don't you want to feel them?" she asked.

"I felt them when I took them out of your suitcase."

"Feel them on me," she said.

"Get into bed. You need sleep," he said.

Kit frowned. "Not sleep. Sex."

"If you get into your bed alone and stay asleep and decide in twenty-four hours you still need sex, I'll help you find it." When the drug was out of her system, she wouldn't request sex. It was an offer he wouldn't need to fulfill.

"Help me find it? I don't need to find it. You can give it to me."

"It's a deal. If you get into bed now, in twenty-four hours, I'll have sex with you if you still feel the same."

Kit climbed onto the bed and smirked at him victoriously. He handed her a bottle of water, which she drank.

"Can I trust you not to leave this room if I step into the bathroom to change?" he asked. He was responsible for her well-being and he already carried a sense he had failed. She had been drugged while he was responsible for her.

"Can I watch?"

"Nothing to see, so no."

She blew out her breath in a huff. "Fine. I'll stay in the room."

Hurrying into the bathroom with dry clothes, he changed as quickly as possible and returned to the room. He braced himself for more tests of his professionalism.

She was kneeling on the bed. "You are really, really sexy. When I first saw you, I thought you might be a model."

"I'm a regular guy."

Kit rolled her eyes and settled back on the mound of pillows at the top of her bed. "You are not regular. How about you come here and let me tell you the ways you are not regular?"

"Our deal was that you stay in your bed alone."

"Fine. You can miss all the fun." She was beneath her covers, wriggling. Kit sat up in bed. "Griffin?"

"Yes?" he asked, bracing himself for another request he couldn't satisfy.

"Why is it so easy for you to say no to me?"

It wasn't easy for him. It was part of his job. He would love to throw care to the wind and sleep with her. But his mission came first and required his focus. "I don't sleep with people involved with my missions."

"Then you're fired," she said.

"You can't fire me. I don't work for you."

"Give me the phone. Let me talk to Connor."

Connor didn't need to hear lust-fueled, drugged ranting. Griffin could handle this. "You're stuck with me."

She grunted in frustration. "My skin feels too sensitive, like I want to be grabbed and left alone at the same time." She climbed out of bed and seized her computer. She opened it and turned it on. In moments, she was typing frantically at the keyboard.

"What are you doing?" he asked.

"Trolling for someone to have sex with."

He grabbed the computer and slammed the lid shut. Not acceptable. "No."

"Why? What would it hurt?" she asked. "I can hide behind an alias."

Why not? He couldn't think of a good reason other than he didn't want her to. He didn't want her to have sex with anyone. He should protect her from terrible drug-induced decisions. Though that wasn't the whole of the reason, he didn't explore those emotions too deeply.

"Griffin, you can't have everything your way."

"Nothing about this is my way," he said, trying to

keep the irritation from his voice. The pent-up desire he felt was getting the best of him. "You can't leave this room to meet up with some stranger." He was doing the right thing. He would not question it.

"I wouldn't have to leave the room. Good old cybersex."

He didn't like either idea. "Why don't I run you a bath?" he asked. A distraction. He mustered his frayed patience.

"My skin is clean," she said in a breathy voice.

"Not to clean you. To relax you."

She moaned again. "A bath. Anything."

He ran a bath, and then called to her. "I'll phone room service and ask for some fresh towels."

She went into the bathroom. He kept the door cracked in case she needed him.

An hour later, she exited the bathroom in a white hotel robe.

Griffin reclined in his bed and ignored the raging hard-on he'd been sporting for the better part of four hours. It would go away. He blew out his breath and counted backward slowly.

Kit sat on the edge of his bed.

"What's the matter? What do you need?" he asked.

She said nothing, but she stood. She let the robe fall off her shoulders, exposing her neck, her upper body, just shy of her breasts. "I'm still in the mood. I have a great feeling about you and me. This could be amazing if you'd let this happen. Stop fighting it. I've been taking care of this myself, but I think you could do a better job." She crawled on top of him and he flipped her off him, onto the mattress. Her soft thigh brushed his legs.

"Get back in your bed," he said.

"I like this bed better."

"Then I'll sleep in the other bed," he said.

She launched herself at him, kissing his neck. "I want to be in the bed with you."

"No." He was tired and her pleas wore on him. His sense of honor prevented him from giving in to her.

"Let's modify our arrangement," she said.

"No."

"Just sleep in the same bed with me. Just hold me," she said.

Gray area. Lying in the same bed, relaxed and pressed together, would lead to sex. "No."

He set her firmly on the ground.

"I know you want to do this," she said.

"I don't," he said. Did his body desperately want the relief of sinking into hers? Of course. But he wouldn't do that. Not to her.

She stilled. "Really?"

"Really." It would go against everything he believed. It would compromise who he was as a man and as an operative.

It was the first time his rejection of her had slowed her down. Was the drug wearing off? She said nothing and returned to her bed.

Twenty minutes later, he heard her gasp and then run into the bathroom. He followed, concerned. She was sitting on the floor of the bathroom, her hair flung forward, gagging into the toilet.

Griffin took a clean white washcloth from the rack in the bathroom and put some cool water on it. He helped her wipe her mouth. He laid another washcloth across the back of her neck. She was covered in sweat.

Kit murmured her thanks. Then she rose onto her knees and leaned over the toilet again. Griffin gathered her hair in his hand and held it.

She gagged again. "What's wrong with me? Is this a typical response to the drug?"

Instead of the flirtatious mewling, her tone was normal. Her body could be getting rid of the drug through any means possible.

"I'll check with Connor." If it was a bad reaction that required medical attention, Griffin wanted to know and take her to the emergency room.

She moaned, but this time, she sounded in pain.

Connor confirmed it was a good sign that the drug was working its way out of her body. "Do you want me to send a doctor over there tonight?" Connor asked.

Griffin asked Kit and she shook her head. "Tomorrow. Doctor tomorrow."

Griffin relayed the message to Connor and then disconnected.

"Can you help me back into bed?" she asked. She was trembling, either from fatigue or cold—he wasn't sure.

He didn't wait for her to struggle to her feet. He carried her to her bed and laid her down. She didn't grab at his shirt and try to pull him into the bed with her. The worst of the drug had passed through her system.

* * *

Kit felt like her head would split open. Had she been drunk last night? Why did she feel this way?

She opened her eyes and remembered she was in a hotel room at Gamer Con. She and Griffin had gone to a rave and then… Kit groaned as she remembered intimate details of the night before. Had she had sex with Griffin? She couldn't remember him on top of her, but she remembered touching him and kissing him.

"Griffin?" Her throat was raw. He was seated by the window, reading.

He rose and came to the side of the bed. "What can I get you?"

"Acetaminophen. Ibuprofen. Water. Coffee."

He nodded to her bedside table. "Let's start with the acetaminophen and water."

She glanced at both set out on a tray. "Was I drunk last night?"

"You were drugged."

Drugged? "But what? By whom?"

"As far as I can tell, some low-life at the rave. Possibly someone looking to take advantage of women. The West Company is reviewing the security tapes and investigating."

Because she and Griffin were attending Gamer Con under aliases, they couldn't file a police report or do anything to draw attention to the situation, which would draw attention to them. "What did I do?" She had some strange memories. Dreams or reality? Did she kiss Griffin?

"You didn't do anything. When I realized what was happening, I brought you back to the hotel room. When you're ready, we have a doctor on stand-by to check you over and make sure you're okay."

If she'd had sex with him and didn't remember it, she would absolutely lose it. "Did we have sex? Like any kind of sex? I remember doing some things…"

His cheeks grew red. "You were solo. I kept you in the room so no one could hurt you. The drug made you really interested in sex. But you managed it on your own."

He had witnessed her acting like a sex-starved lunatic. "Wonderful."

"The drug is called rapture. No inhibitions and too much serotonin and adrenaline. You couldn't help how you felt or behaved. From what I read about it online, you got through it like a champ."

Kit looked away to hide her embarrassment. She grabbed her phone. "I need to know more about this."

"Don't internet-research it. You'll get freaked out. Do you want to take today and rest?"

"Why would I get freaked out?" she asked.

"Not everyone who takes rapture, willingly or unwillingly, ends up safe."

"Then I should thank you for looking out for me," she said.

"Just doing my job."

Except it was so much more. He watched over her. He protected her. It felt amazing to be in such capable, committed hands. "I guess we need to refocus." Gamer Con was a limited day conference. Kit couldn't spend the day hiding because she felt ill and was embarrassed about her behavior. Griffin seemed indifferent to it. Maybe it wasn't a big deal. "I feel fine now. I want to track down at least one or two of the hackers I know to help me with the Locker."

"You set the pace."

Kit took a shower and changed into street clothes. After the doctor from the West Company visited and confirmed she was fine, but advised her to drink fluids and rest, she felt better about the whole ordeal.

"We need to change into our costumes," Kit said.

"We're not dressing as the vampire people again?" Griffin asked.

She couldn't play that video game again or hear the word *vampire* without thinking about how sexy Griffin had looked in his costume or how it had felt to rub against him. From what she remembered, he had been kind but firm against anything transpiring between them. It was a compliment to his sense of honor and a blow to her ego.

She couldn't even seduce a man while she was blatantly throwing herself at one.

"We have new costumes for today," she said, wishing she had ordered dragons or head-to-toe ninja outfits. Although Griffin would look unbearably hot in either, at least she wouldn't feel so exposed.

"Good. My vampire costume is still wet."

"From what?" As the question left her mouth, she remembered. She had asked him to shower with her and he had, wearing his clothes. Humiliation burned through her. She wasn't a seductress. But standing fully clothed in the shower spoke to his disinterest. Could she use the word *repulsion*?

Griffin might have been trying to be an honorable man by keeping his distance, but if Kit had half the appeal her sister had, he would have failed.

She handed him the garment bag with his costume, but he didn't open it.

He cleared his throat. "Do you want to talk about what happened between us?"

Not on her last day. "I'd rather not relive it."

"Is your memory okay? Do you remember last night?"

It was foggy. "Bits and pieces."

"You have nothing to worry about. Nothing happened."

He was putting a fine point on it. "You saw me naked."

"I did."

She could not look him in the eye. "How do you feel about last night?"

"Guilty. I should have noticed someone touching you with the drug," he said.

What about when they'd been alone and she'd been throwing herself at him? He didn't seem like the type to have a laugh at her expense, but was he disgusted? Angry? Frustrated that he'd been saddled with her? She was embarrassed enough to let him leave and be assigned to another operative. "Do you want to call Connor and ask him to assign me to someone else?"

He appeared confused. "Is that what you want?"

Kit leveled with him. "I'm embarrassed."

"No need," he said.

His statement didn't change anything. Could she continue on with him as her protector knowing she had made a fool of herself? He might think about it every time he looked at her. Would she think differently of her? His phone buzzed and he answered it.

"Right. Okay. We'll be careful. Thanks, Connor."

"What's happened?" she asked.

"I have some bad news. Connor's learned that you weren't the only woman who was exposed to rapture last night. Every woman who's reported she was drugged is a brunette, same height and build as you, and has similar features."

Was she being targeted specifically, or did the attacker have some bizarre fascination with brunettes? "Are the others okay?" She'd had Griffin to protect her, but not every woman would have been as lucky.

"One woman is in the hospital with dehydration and alcohol poisoning, and the drug in her system. The rest are okay."

"Do you think this has anything to do with Incognito?"

"Someone at the rave could have tried to lure you away and question you to find out if you are Lotus. Under the effects of the drug, you would have gone anywhere with anyone who was promising sex."

She winced as another memory struck her. The promise of sex. Griffin had told her he would sleep with her if she still wanted to after twenty-four hours. Did he remember that? She wouldn't bring it up.

"There's a security conference in Washington, DC,

this week. Connor has intel that Incognito is looking for you there, as well."

Kit ran a shaky hand through her hair. "Do we need to leave? Is it too dangerous to be here?"

"We have work to do to protect the Locker. If this is the best place for you to assemble your team, I'll keep you safe."

Kit had to forget about what had happened during her drug-induced failed seduction. At least it had been a failed seduction. How would she have lived with herself if she'd had to tell Griffin that she was a novice at everything in the bedroom? It was a scenario in which being under the influence would not have helped her.

Her inhibitions would have been lower, but she wouldn't have been able to think as clearly about what she was doing. She needed to think through the steps. Like when she was designing a software program or playing a video game, she liked to see the big picture first and break it down into smaller tasks.

The big picture with Griffin was unclear. He was her bodyguard, protector, but not a friend. He'd been good to her the night before, and he was keeping their boundaries firm and clear. She wouldn't presume an emotional relationship between them, but she was attached to him. Once before she had made the mistake of believing a man's kindness to her was affection. But that situation had been a disaster, and it wouldn't happen again.

Chapter 6

Kit was struggling with what had happened the night before, but Griffin stayed cool and casual about it. He had seen some strange situations in his career, and this was another of them. No big deal.

Except it was a big deal to him. Images of Kit naked had been burned into his brain. Her pink lips, her soft skin and her curvy frame rubbing against him were too memorable, replaying too often.

Disguises or not, the longer he and Kit lingered at this conference, the more likely she would be recognized. Losing focus while Incognito was looking for her was dangerous. The costumes helped their cover, but someone would figure out who she was. Her real name, her former hacker name and her contributions to the Locker being classified hadn't stopped Incognito from kidnapping members of the team. Brunettes who looked like Kit had been targeted. Someone had a description of her, maybe even a picture. They had attacked her at her sister's party. They knew far too much for Griffin to rest easy.

Kit's Rainbow Sparkle character's outfit was described by the name. She adjusted the glitter-covered mask over her face. It accented her deep brown eyes, and Griffin had trouble not staring at her. He needed to watch the space around her. As last night had proven, someone could get close enough to hurt her.

His costume was for a character named Dragonfly. Dragonfly's outfit was navy velvet pants and a white button-down shirt. It was not a look he liked.

Kit led him to the lobby bar, where a social event was scheduled. It was loud and almost everyone had a phone in their hand, talking and typing, chatting and multitasking.

Kit was no exception. "I'm looking for a hacker named Evasion. I heard from a mutual friend she's here. She hasn't responded to my messages."

"How do you know her?" Griffin asked.

"We taught a class together. An online class," Kit said.

Griffin imagined it was the type of class the authorities would have loved to be invited to but were likely excluded from.

"What does she look like?" he asked, surveying the crowd.

"Never met her. On the insides of her wrists, she has a tattoo of jesters, like on playing cards. She complained about them when she was first inked because they slowed down her typing for a few days."

It was warm enough that most people had exposed wrists. Griffin searched as they moved through the crowd. Kit drew to a stop. She whirled and looked up at him with huge eyes.

"Find her?"

She shook her head. "I see someone who might recognize me."

Griffin slipped his arm around her, shielding her face against him and moving her in the opposite direction. Her costume was good, but he couldn't risk it.

Kit stopped and pushed him slightly. "Maybe I'm overreacting. He could be someone I can trust."

Unlikely. If he was a known associate of Lotus, Incognito might have already put out the word they were looking for her and offering a hefty reward. "We can't trust anyone."

Kit licked her lower lip. "This person we can."

"How do you know?"

"I can trust him." She sounded more confident, and the alarm in her voice was gone.

Maybe it was the slight breeziness of her voice or the awe when she spoke about him, but Griffin had the sense she was holding something back. "Details, Kit, or we're leaving."

Kit pressed a hand over her stomach. "I shouldn't be nervous. He's a member of the military. He's very capable. Strong."

Irrational jealousy poked at him. "You have a personal relationship with him?" Griffin asked, not liking that idea in the least.

"We were, we are…something. Not friends exactly. Not colleagues, either. I don't have a word for it."

Lovers? Friends with benefits? "You want to talk to him. Can he help you now?"

She inclined her head. "Not technically. He's keyed into this world. He might know something and if he doesn't, I should warn him that Incognito is active."

"Does he need to know about that?" Griffin asked. "If he was involved with the project and he's with the military, he would have been apprised of the situation."

"He wasn't directly involved. He served as part of the security team in a no-explanations-given capacity. I'll talk to him. I want to talk to him."

"I can't let you approach him in public. If he says your name and someone overhears it, our cover is blown." Their already shaky cover.

"Please, Griffin. Don't make me tell you the whole story. Just understand that I need to talk to him and we can trust him."

Griffin looked into her pleading eyes and relented. "Give me a minute to work out a plan. Maybe you can talk somewhere private."

Kit inhaled. "Alone?"

He had a visceral reaction to the idea. "I would be there."

Kit brought her hands together and wrung them. Griffin tried to understand. Did this man make her happy or nervous? She was acting like she was meeting an old boyfriend. Was that their relationship? Something that had started while Kit was working on the Locker and had ended over professional ethics or logistics?

Formulating a plan, Griffin led Kit to the patio outside the bar. It was surrounded by a wrought iron fence with no access from the street.

It was hot, and the shade from an awning provided only a slight amount of cooling. Kit sat at the one table half in the shade.

"Tell me which one he is," Griffin said.

She lifted her hand and pointed. "Him."

Griffin turned to see a man in a starched polo shirt and khakis stepping onto the patio. Griffin's hand went to his gun.

"Kit?" the man asked, smiling at her. He strode to her, never taking his eyes off her.

Kit glanced at Griffin before standing and greeting the other man. A mix of curiosity and jealousy struck Griffin.

They embraced, and Kit closed her eyes when he hugged her. He was most definitely her former lover. He knew her real name. What else did he know? Had she shared secrets with him while they shared a pillow?

After a brief exchange of pleasantries, Kit gestured to Griffin. "Lawrence, this is my friend Michael. Michael, Lawrence."

Griffin was pleased she hadn't given his real name. He shook the other man's hand.

Kit gestured for Lawrence to sit across from her. "What are you doing here?"

Lawrence sat and adjusted his chair, moving it closer to Kit. "We're looking for you."

Griffin was prepared to disable Lawrence if he made a move against Kit. Military man or not, Griffin has his orders.

Kit appeared nervous and clasped her hands in her lap. "Don't use my name," Kit warned him. "I still don't want to be found. Who is 'we'?"

"I'm here with Zoya. We heard the team was being hunted."

"Are you safe?" Kit asked.

Lawrence laughed with an edge of nervousness about it. "You don't have to worry about us. I'm always carrying a weapon. I look out for Zoya."

Kit flinched. "Where is she now?"

Who was Zoya? Griffin didn't recall her name from the profiles he'd been given from the West Company.

"She is safe. Don't worry. We're worried about you."

Kit adjusted her mask and tipped it back off her face. "Lawrence, we shouldn't be seen together." She looked over her shoulder at the door to the hotel. She had more to say, but she stopped speaking. Kit did that often enough. Why didn't she speak her mind? Now was her chance to talk to this character.

"Let's have dinner tonight in my room. We can talk more then," Lawrence said.

The intense expression on his face unnerved Griffin.

"Talk about what?" Griffin asked. They were not at the conference to socialize and catch up with old friends for the sport of it.

Lawrence frowned at him. "I know what has been going on. I have information you may find useful."

Information or rumors?

Kit touched the ends of her hair. "We can meet. Michael will need to join us."

Lawrence took Kit's hands, and Griffin stifled a growl. "You don't trust me?" Lawrence asked.

Kit looked at their hands. "I do, but Michael trusts no one."

Kit said Lawrence could be trusted, but Griffin didn't accept that at face value. He would have the West Company dig around about Lawrence and Zoya. If they were working with Incognito or had a brief association with them, they were the enemy. "Come on. We need to go," Griffin said. Being outside for too long would draw attention. Griffin didn't want their pictures taken or anyone to grow curious enough to look twice.

"Tonight. Six o'clock. Room eighteen twelve," Lawrence said.

Kit glanced at Griffin for approval.

"Fine," Griffin said. Kit stood, and Griffin guided her away from Lawrence.

When they were out of earshot, Griffin lowered his mouth to her ear. "Are you sure we can trust him?"

"Yes."

"What about Zoya?" Griffin asked.

"She's his girlfriend. Fiancée. Wife. One of those." Kit sounded contemplative.

Griffin didn't like it. He texted Lawrence's and Zoya's names to Kate West for a more thorough investigation. Kate would dig up any skeletons in their closets.

"We'll keep searching for your friend. Your other friend," Griffin said, wanting to keep them on track.

If Kit was his distraction, Lawrence was hers. He'd prefer if they stayed away from him, but Kit had other ideas.

"Tell me more about the hackers we're looking for," Griffin said.

Kit had a short list of hackers she wanted to contact. She was being careful reaching out to people over the computer, worried that someone who knew her as Lotus would figure out she was at Gamer Con and connect her online persona with her real one.

If Incognito was aware of who she was, so were others.

"In addition to Evasion, I'm looking for a guy who goes by the name Swift," Kit said.

"Is he a fast typist?" Griffin asked.

"Yes." Most hackers were. Swift's nickname came from his ability to get into and out of a secure site faster than most. Kit wouldn't out his crimes to Griffin. Though Swift's bio was in an online encyclopedia, Kit respected the privacy of her fellow hackers. She played by the unwritten rules of a hacker's code of honor, and that meant keeping the authorities out of the loop whenever possible. In this case, Griffin was the authorities.

Like most of the people she was close to in the hacker community, Swift was also her personal friend. In fact, Swift was the first and only man she'd had a serious relationship with. She and Swift had many common interests. Beyond gaming, they loved security protocols and had enjoyed lively debates about the best methods to secure a server or a website or a personal laptop.

"Do I need to be worried that he knows about your involvement with…"

Griffin didn't need to say "with the Locker."

"He knows nothing about that. He knows me only as Orchid. I met him online after I was finished with that project."

Concern creased the corners of Griffin's eyes. "Tell me more about Swift."

Griffin didn't have time to vet Swift. Kit gave him the quick and dirty. "He's someone I used to date. My most serious relationship." Swift would be easier to find since he had registered for a booth to sell portable laptop desks and had used his online name for the promo.

"Bad idea to bring an old lover into this," Griffin said.

Kit wasn't sure she'd given Griffin the right information about Swift. *Lover* implied intimacies she hadn't shared with him. The end of her relationship with Swift had been dramatic, but the sting of his betrayal was long gone. "He doesn't hold a grudge. He cheated on me. If anyone should be mad over how the relationship ended, it's me."

"You're not mad at him and harboring residual anger?" Griffin asked.

"No." She had been at first. But dragging around resentment was harder on her than on Swift.

Kit glanced at Griffin's face. He revealed no discernible emotion. Describing his stare as vacant wouldn't have been accurate. He was watching, observing and thinking a few steps ahead. No emotion, though.

"He said he needed physical contact." Why was she still babbling to Griffin about Swift? It didn't matter why their relationship had ended. It was likely not one reason. Online relationships were as complex and difficult to navigate as in-person ones, sometimes more so because the distance left more leeway for lies.

"What does that mean?" Griffin asked.

Online relationships operated under their own rules. Griffin couldn't understand it, or worse, he would judge her.

She'd give Griffin the ten-second explanation. "Swift and I met online. We lived a thousand miles apart. We didn't meet in person. We had planned to meet, but we broke up before then." She hadn't rushed to meet him. Meeting a new person was anxiety-causing. A disruption in her daily routine was stressful enough to have her put the trip off with excuses for several months.

Griffin blinked at her. "Your most serious relationship was with someone you didn't see in person?"

He sounded confused, and she had to explain and justify what she and Swift had. "We talked every day. Multiple times a day. It was intimate. And we had cybersex." She added the last statement in case Griffin thought she was too boring.

"What is that, like sexting?" he asked.

"Similar. But we talked over the instant messenger service on our private servers."

"He would type to you and you would type to him." He still sounded bewildered.

"Right."

"You didn't want the real thing?" Griffin asked.

His question ignited her defensiveness. "What we had was the real thing. What wasn't real about it?"

Griffin inclined his head. He didn't sound judgmental, just like he was trying to understand. "How do you have a relationship with someone that doesn't include holding his hand and touching him and kissing him?"

Most of her relationships could be described as not involving touching. "We had emotional intimacy. It was modern."

"If modern dating means more time with my hands on a keyboard and less time with my hands on my girlfriend, then forget it."

Based on how women looked at Griffin, he'd had his share of interested partners and had likely taken a few home with him. "It's stressful to meet someone new. It's stressful to go on dates."

"The upside is huge. When it works, it's amazing," Griffin said.

Given her behavior the night before, he had the wrong idea about her. She hadn't had sex with a man. "I suppose."

"I don't like first dates, either, but sometimes they can be great. A little ice breaking and then it's smooth sailing. Instead of pushing through some awkwardness, you avoid it?" Griffin asked.

Her sister had accused her of the same thing, telling her she needed to leave her room, go out and meet men. Kit had tried, but she was better at talking over the computer. "I tried online dating, but it was too hard to move past the online part. I'm more comfortable conversing with a couple of computers between us."

"You've been doing well in person here."

She felt safe at Gamer Con, knowing she was among people who were similar to her and Griffin was keeping her safe. "This has taken me outside my comfort zone in a zillion ways. I'm doing this because I know lives are at stake."

"Then this Swift is some Casanova of the computer?" Griffin asked.

"He's good with words, yes. He is also able to break most security protocols and exploit almost any piece of software." Which would be handy if they needed to destroy the copy of the Locker.

"But he doesn't like touching women." Griffin's lip twitched, fighting a smile.

Kit rolled her eyes. "He does. That was one of our problems."

"Lead the way to this master of the computer who

somehow seduces women without being in the same room with them. Maybe he can teach me a thing or two."

"I get the feeling few men could teach you much about women. You seem to handle us just fine. You handled me fine last night." She blushed, the words coming out wrong. "I mean, you kept me from further injuring myself."

"Doing my job," he said and cleared his throat.

Except when he went out of his way to assist her, it felt like he was doing more than a job. He was being a friend to her.

Swift was easy to find. He wasn't in hiding, and by asking around, Kit was pointed to the main sales area, where vendors had set up displays to demo their latest games, equipment and computer accessories.

Kit spotted Swift from thirty feet away. She stilled, peering at him from around another stall. He looked as she remembered over their video chats. He was tall, maybe as tall as Griffin, but slender. He dressed as she would have expected, well-worn jeans and a bright hooded sweatshirt. He wore his black hair long in the front and shaved short around the sides and back. His bangs hung over his right eye and he flicked his head to move them.

Swift was speaking to another man. He laughed at something the man said and turned his head in her direction. She ducked behind the stall.

"What's the matter?" Griffin asked. "Changed your mind?"

Not exactly changed her mind. She was filled with self-conscious thoughts. Swift had dumped her because she wasn't interesting enough. She wasn't sexy enough. If he had wanted to be with her, he would have driven to see her when she was ready. He would have invited her to his place. He would have set up a weekend for them at a romantic bed-and-breakfast. The list of what she had wanted from the relationship and hadn't gotten ran through her head.

She hadn't been aware she had wanted those things. Wasn't she happy being in an online relationship? Wasn't that ideal for her? "Talking to him is harder than I thought. It's been enough time that it shouldn't bother me, but I feel weak."

"Weak?" Griffin asked, concern in his voice.

"He's in a position of power, and I'm begging him for a favor."

The expression on Griffin's face said he didn't like that much at all. "You're not begging this clown for anything. If he wants to help with one of the most prestigious computer security projects on the planet, then fine, he has an in. But if he doesn't, then forget him."

Kit straightened her shoulders and smoothed her hair. She checked that her costume was in place and approached slowly. She felt like she had rocks in her shoes and she willed herself not to trip, stutter or otherwise make a fool of herself.

If she had some of her sister's grace or her mother's confidence or her brother's charm, she could have used it. Her mother half-jokingly said that she'd been given the lion's share of the brains in the family, but none of the beauty. Childhood teasing from her mother that still hurt.

Her mother hadn't understood why Kit didn't want to attend her high school prom. Kit had been too embarrassed to admit that no one had asked her to be his date. Her mother didn't understand why Kit hadn't gone on an island vacation for spring break when she was in college. No friends had included her in their plans. A lifetime of social rejections that led to computers being at the top of the list for the best place for Kit to socialize. Behind the screen of a computer, she was safe and all anyone could see was her intellect. That had been her best—maybe only—strength, and she wielded it like a sword online.

Her intellect didn't translate well in real life, especially when it was hidden beneath her awkwardness and stuttering.

"Hey, are you okay?" Griffin asked, taking her shoulders and forcing her to look at him.

"I can do this." Speaking to Swift in person for the first time was a hurdle she hadn't crossed during their relationship, but she could handle it now. She had Griffin with her, and this wasn't about her insecurities and fears. This was bigger. If Incognito gained control of the Locker, Kit knew the consequences could be dire.

Meeting Griffin's gaze, she lost her train of thought. She could have lost herself in his deep green eyes. He had this serious and concerned way of looking at her that made her feel both vulnerable and protected.

What did Swift see when he looked at her? What did other people see? "Do people assume you're all brawn and no brains?" she asked.

Broad, sinewy shoulders lifted in a shrug. "Probably." He seemed indifferent to the idea.

"Does that bother you?"

He shook his head. "It doesn't matter what others think about me."

A lot of people claimed they didn't care what others thought about them. She had made the same statement many times, but deep down, she did care. However, Griffin was confident in himself and his abilities. He was strong and smart, and he owned it.

"It matters to me what Swift thinks." She would leave it at that. In her dream world, Swift would see her and realize what he was missing. When she had confronted him with the evidence of his cheating, he had called her a stalker, and they hadn't spoken since. Maybe now he would apologize for cheating on her and admit he missed their conversations. Then she could reject him and regain some of her dignity.

Swift might not be her favorite person, but he was talented. He could help counter Incognito's attempts at taking control of the Locker.

Griffin glanced over at Swift. "If you don't want to talk to him, then forget it. Plenty of other recruits in this hotel."

Swift's computer security countermeasures were legendary. "Swift has the skills to help us. He's the best at what he does." That had to take priority over her personal feelings and insecurities.

Griffin set his hand on her lower back. "I'm right behind you."

Swift knew she was Orchid, but she had never confided in him about her work with the Locker or her former persona, Lotus.

Though having Griffin close would have felt good, she wanted to do this alone. She had to prove to herself she had grown from the experience. "You can hang back. I can do this." Swift might think Griffin was a fed and get spooked.

Taking a deep breath and wishing she was a little drunk for this, she strolled to see him. When he caught her eye, she waved. He glanced at her, turned to the guys on either side of him and said something to them. They snickered, and her confidence took a bullet to the heart. She almost lost her nerve, but she gritted her teeth, lifted her chin and pinned back her shoulders. Griffin was watching. She would not turn and run.

Swift sauntered to her, hands shoved in his front jeans pockets. His orange hoodie was baggy, and he leaned forward, hunching his shoulders.

This was a simple conversation, and to botch this would be humiliating. If she were rejected by the people she considered acquaintances and associates, who else did she have in her life?

"Hey, Swift." She tried to hide the nervous shaking in her hands. She adjusted her mask so he could see her face.

His eyes lit. "Kit. You look good." He moved her wig's bangs to the side.

When his fingers brushed her forehead, she leaned away.

She didn't return the compliment. Though his appearance was something she dug, since meeting Griffin, she decided something—and someone—else interested her. This was about a job, and her previous attraction to Swift was irrelevant.

"I need to talk with you about something," Kit said. She wished she had a better opening line than that.

He folded his arms over his chest. "If this is about what happened between us, I don't want to have a big fight in public over it. It was years ago. It's over. I've moved on."

His words stung more than they should have. "It's not about our past," she said, feeling embarrassed and then mad at herself for feeling embarrassed. Why should she feel bad? She wasn't the one who had cheated. "I wanted to talk to you about a job."

"I don't give security consults without signing a contract first and being put on retainer," he said.

This could be the biggest job of his career. "Not even for an old friend?"

"Friends? Is that your way of trying to pin me down? I'm dating a lot of women. I don't want to settle down," he said and patted her on the shoulder.

"I'm not asking you to date me," she said.

"You want to go somewhere and have cybersex?"

He laughed. "Because I need a woman who will do more than talk about sex."

Heat flamed up her neck.

Why was Swift being a jerk to her?

Kit felt hot tears coming to her eyes. He was humiliating her. People were walking by and looking at them. She hated feeling this way. This was a prime example of why she preferred online life. Online, she was quick-witted, and she could sign off and walk away from her computer. Here, she had nowhere to go, and her tongue felt too big for her mouth. Quick retorts weren't spilling out. Running away was pathetic, and while it was unlikely that anyone would remember the woman in the rainbow wig, similar to dozens of others, she felt on display. And he was making a mockery of her.

"I'm only interested in talking with you about a job," she said. She gave herself credit for getting that much out and staying calm and collected. She hadn't stuttered and she had maintained her professionalism, even if what he deserved was a kick in the shins.

"Unless it's a blow job, I'm not interested."

Kit could not believe he was being such a colossal jerk to her. "Why are you acting like this?" Her face was hot and her hands were trembling. No chance of hiding it.

"I'm not acting like anything. I'm trying to make it clear I'm not interested. You're not getting the message. I've got other women. Until you can learn to interact with men and do more than talk about sex, you'll be alone. It's pathetic that you came here looking for me and pretending you have some job to offer. Why are you really here? To get back at me?"

Kit swallowed. She'd walk away. Wasting time with Swift wasn't getting her anywhere, and she didn't know if she could work with him. Other people at the conference had the skills to help her. Maybe they weren't as notorious or experienced, but she couldn't stand working with Swift if this was his attitude toward her.

"Just forget I said anything," Kit said.

Swift rolled his eyes. "Don't be dramatic. If you want, I'll let you give me a hand job behind the display. Although I would prefer if you'd use that mouth. Tell me, do you feel like taking an oral exam?"

Kit shook her head to clear the angry thoughts running through it. His ego was in need of validation, and she wouldn't stand here and let him use her to get it.

Griffin was at her side, moving so quietly and quickly she hadn't heard him approach. He slipped his arm around her shoulders, and where his skin brushed hers, she would have sworn she was on fire.

"Hey, baby, what's taking so long?" He pivoted her toward him and delivered the most life-altering, soul-shaking kiss. She melted against him, and thank God his strong arms were banded around her waist, because she would have crumpled to the floor. His mouth opened hers and she was his, willing and ready. He could have stripped off her clothes and she wouldn't have protested.

His lips massaged hers, and his tongue stroked against hers in an erotically charged manner. Griffin pulled her hips to his. Tucked against him, she felt divine. If this was a precursor to sex, she had waited far too long to try it out.

The kiss was over in seconds, and he kept his arm around her possessively. Kit couldn't engage her brain. Her lips were burning and her body tingled. She wanted more of what he had delivered.

"You must be Sniff," Griffin said.

When she finally tore her eyes away from Griffin's beautiful face and lips, she leaned against him, partly because she was into her role of his lover and partly because it felt amazing to be with him. Had Griffin felt the soul-shaking energy, too? Was every kiss that amazing?

"Swift," he corrected Griffin, narrowing his eyes. "Who are you?"

"Her boyfriend who is tired of waiting. If you want to tell him about the job at the law firm, tell him. Then come on." He swiveled his hips into her, and a ripple of anticipation ripped through her. "I have things I want to do before you rush off to another seminar."

Griffin was warning her off from telling Swift about the reason for her approach and giving her a simple exit. Dashing off for sex was a great way to end the conversation. She didn't have to pretend she was into the idea. Sex with Griffin would be an explosive, mind-altering way to spend an hour.

The cherry on top of that fantasy was, of course, Swift believing she had moved on and had a hot, attentive boyfriend with whom she had wild sex.

"Never mind. It's not work that interests him," Kit said.

Swift held up his hand. "Wait, I didn't say I wasn't interested."

It was exactly what he'd said.

Griffin's thumb rubbed her hip. "I'm not crazy about you working with a man, anyway. If you work exclusively with me, we can work naked. Much more fun."

Swift looked between them. "You two are a couple? How? Are you using her for her computer skills?"

Griffin laughed. "I love her computer skills. But I don't choose my lovers based on their ability to type on a machine. I have a more strenuous and detailed selection process."

Swift folded his arms over his chest. "Dude, do you realize she prefers cybersex to sex?"

Griffin gave Swift a thin smile and then kissed Kit on the cheek. "I haven't found that to be the case. She is fantastic and smart and beautiful."

Swift sent Kit an appraising look.

Griffin steered her away. "Later, Swiss."

Chapter 7

They left Swift standing slack jawed. Kit was struck by gratitude, lust and excitement. For her ex to believe she was hot in bed, and hot in bed with a man like Griffin, was the best revenge. As they walked away, Griffin's hand moved to her rear end. "He's still watching us," he said as if she required an explanation.

"Why did you say that to him?" Kit asked.

"He's a smug little prick, and he was taking joy in talking down to you. I would have hit him, but it seemed wiser if I assumed the role of satisfied and hungry lover as opposed to jealous psycho."

"Why lovers at all?" Kit asked.

"Because a man and woman traveling together and staying in the same hotel room are likely lovers and that supports our cover. The other reason is far more petty. I wanted him to know he had lost you, and I wanted him to be insanely covetous."

"Why did you kiss me?" she asked, touching her lips.

"I wanted to infuriate him to the point that he took a swing at me so I could swing back, but no luck."

"He wouldn't hit you. He'd be crazy," Kit said. Standing side by side, Griffin had at least five inches on Swift and a few dozen pounds of lean muscle mass. He was almost twice as wide, shoulder to shoulder.

Griffin's kiss had been unexpected. She was still reeling. Her libido was running rampant, devising a plan to coerce him to do it again. She was assigning a lot of meaning to it because it had been significant to her. "That was my first kiss."

He faced her, and he seemed confused. "With me? I know."

"With anyone." It had bothered her for a long time to lag behind her peers in sexual experiences, but after a while, she rationalized that someone had to be on the bell curve to the far, far left in the completely inexperienced zone. She shared the space with nuns and eunuchs.

"It was a great kiss," he said.

Griffin had taken possession of her mouth, and she had loved every second of it. "I want you to kiss me again." Bold, hungry words. Would he comply?

"He's not watching us," Griffin said.

They were a distance from the sales displays,

standing near lines of empty tables, likely set up for an event later in the day.

She didn't want this kiss to be about Swift. It was about Griffin. "I don't care about him."

Griffin drew her close. "I can't kiss you again. Sex in the field is a great release, but it's a mistake."

"One brief moment won't change anything," Kit said, rubbing her body against his. She increased the pressure. If she moved just right, could she seduce him? Being this turned on without an outlet had to damage her brain. She couldn't think about anything except Griffin and his hands and lips on her.

Griffin ran his hand down her cheek. "It can't lead anywhere, and that's where the trouble starts. My role in your life is to protect you, and I don't know how temporary that role is."

She set her hands on his hips, not wanting him to turn away or change his mind. "You are protecting me. If you don't kiss me, I'll kiss you."

"This is still rapture talking," Griffin said.

"It isn't. You kissed me and you touched me and you started something."

Capitulation in his eyes. Her heart lit up, knowing he wanted to kiss her. A man like Griffin didn't do anything without wanting to.

Griffin kissed her again, softly this time, as if she were something to be cherished. Kit closed her eyes and let the sensations of his lips on hers arouse every nerve in her body. She didn't fight it. Diving deep into the kiss, she heard a moan. It took her a moment to realize it was she making the noise.

Griffin broke the kiss. "Kit, if you keep doing that, you will not like where this leads."

Doing what? She opened her eyes. "We were kissing."

"Yes, but you were moaning. Loudly. Which I was enjoying too much. We need boundaries. Someone might see us."

"We're undercover as lovers. Let's go deep undercover. So deep that we live the lie." Kit touched the side of his face, because she had wanted to for so long and didn't know if she would have another chance. She had imagined what her first kiss would be like. The second was more what she'd pictured.

With Griffin, a kiss could escalate into sex in a split second. They could have skipped a hundred incremental touches in between and she would have gone over the summit with him. "Thank you for what you did with Swift. Thank you for kissing me like that."

Griffin's shoulders lowered a few centimeters. "You don't have to thank me. I enjoyed it."

Had he? Which part? Putting Swift in his place or the kiss? Kit was too nervous to ask.

"According to Kate West, Lawrence is clean. His service record and his security file indicate no problems. No sanctions against him, and he has never been accused of crimes against the United States. He has no known associations with any hackers except for his fiancée, Zoya," Griffin said. "Zoya has a few gray areas on her record. She worked for a technology terrorist group when she was in her twenties. She built viruses and sold them to the highest bidder through an underground hacker auction site."

Kit had known about Zoya's ties to a hacker group that operated within the United States. Zoya's father had been a founding member, and Kit had the impression Zoya hadn't been totally on board with the family pastime. She had been cleared to work on the Locker, having passed the security, psychological and intellectual tests. One bad decision didn't mean she should be blacklisted.

"Did you want Shade to find something bad about Lawrence?" Kit asked.

"No."

He wasn't telling her something. "You sound annoyed."

"He's a security risk," Griffin said.

Griffin's constant concern. "Lawrence and Zoya are safe."

"How would you describe your relationship with them?" Griffin asked.

"We are friendly." She added the *-ly* because she wouldn't call them friends. They weren't close. They didn't trade texts and emails. After going their separate ways at the end of the Locker project, they had followed their debriefing instructions and hadn't located or contacted each other.

"Lawrence asked you to dinner. That implies a friendship," Griffin said.

Kit wasn't sure how to respond. "We have a rocky past."

"A dangerous past?"

Kit shook her head. "I misinterpreted something."

"What does that mean?"

She didn't want to tell this embarrassing story, but if she didn't, Griffin wouldn't relent and allow the dinner. "I thought Lawrence and I were friends, maybe more, but he made it clear he did not think of me in those terms." It wasn't the first time and it likely wouldn't be the last time a man rejected her.

"You must hang out with half-wits," he said.

Kit jolted. "Are you making fun of me?"

"I'm making fun of the men in your life who don't see who you are. They see the computer expertise and not the package it comes in."

Except for keeping her safe so she could help with the Locker project, Griffin didn't seem to care about what she knew about cybersecurity.

Griffin glanced at the clock on the table and frowned. "Let's go now."

"It's too early."

"We set the timeline. If anyone overheard our plans, they could be waiting for you. If someone hacked Lawrence's calendar and knows you're arriving, we'll be ambushed."

"Lawrence knows how to handle security."

Griffin stood and nodded toward the door. "We'll go now. I let you make the calls about computer security. You let me make the calls about physical security."

Kit and Griffin took the elevator to Lawrence's room, stopping a few floors above and taking the stairs the rest of the way. Lawrence and Zoya were staying on the floor comprised of executive suites. Lawrence liked fine things, good wine, luxury travel and great clothes. Kit had admired his good taste, until he'd told her of his plans to use his vacation time to travel to an all-inclusive resort with a civilian he had been dating. Kit had thought he was interested in her. She had misread him completely.

His casual conversation about his plans had stung more because she hadn't been allowed to take a vacation. She had been confined to the base for the duration of the Locker project.

The hall was quiet. Conference attendees were socializing or eating in one of the hotel's eight restaurants.

Griffin gestured for her to stand to the side of the door. Griffin tapped on the door once.

The door opened, and Lawrence swung a gun into his face.

Griffin was trained to react to a threat. He grabbed the gun, pushing it up and away from him and Kit. Griffin tore the gun from Lawrence's hands and leveled it at him.

Lawrence held up his hands and backed away. "Just being careful."

"It isn't a good idea to point a gun in my face." Griffin put the safety on and set the gun on the dresser. Lawrence was lucky. Griffin was trained to kill people who threatened him. The gun was a threat. He had neutralized Lawrence too easily. Maybe the other man had let go of the gun once he saw it was Griffin, or maybe Lawrence had lost his edge.

Griffin had a bad feeling about this gathering. It was off to a shaky start. "Kit, it's clear." Griffin didn't want her lingering in the hall.

Kit slipped into the room. The expression on her face when she saw Lawrence ignited a bolt of jealousy. What was the big deal about this guy? Griffin didn't see it.

A red-haired woman stepped in from the other room. She was tall and wore a gray sweatshirt and black athletic pants, which accented her lean build.

"Lotus," the woman said.

Kit didn't smile. "Zoya."

Lawrence stepped between them and slid his arm around Zoya's waist. "We've had our differences in the past, but we need to work together now. We're all in danger."

Zoya put her hand on Lawrence's chest. Kit looked from Zoya's hand and then to the floor.

"We've been staking out the conference, looking for members of the team," Lawrence said. "Anyone who worked on the Locker could be drawn to this place. Probably using a different name, but we might recognize them."

"We're here for the same reason," Kit said.

Zoya's eyebrows lifted. "You travel with a personal bodyguard now?"

Kit ignored the question. "What's the plan?"

"To counter Incognito. They have pieces of the Locker and they have probably made copies," Lawrence said. "I want to destroy the copies. I have a lead on where they might be, but I'd need your help to break in."

Kit looked between the two of them. "Okay."

Lawrence inclined his head. "That's it? Okay?"

"Give me a few hours to make some plans and get the equipment I need. Then we'll go on the offensive against Incognito."

Kit was in a bad mood. Seeing Zoya and Lawrence together left her feeling small and unwanted, like a rowdy child at a formal dinner party.

She and Griffin were en route to the local Tech Buy to pick up equipment. Shopping for computers and devices normally thrilled her, but she was distracted and irritated. Why did Zoya and Lawrence have to look so in love? Why were they still together? Had Lawrence told Zoya about the time Kit had thrown herself at him? Had they shared a laugh about it at her expense?

"You said our cover was lovers," Kit said.

"It is," Griffin said, changing lanes.

"Then let's actually do it."

He glanced at her. "Do what? Have sex?"

Why did men treat sex with her like the least desirable option on a menu? She was the liverwurst and Brussels sprouts on a menu of Kobe steak and truffles. From what she had read, men liked sex. They liked it even when they weren't crazy about the woman they were sleeping with. "You said if I still wanted it after twenty-four hours, you would."

She was glad they were in the car and she didn't have to look at him directly. The promise he'd made her had been to keep her calm when she was drugged, but the promise should have held water regardless of how it was made.

"You remembered that? I was attempting to prevent you from making a mistake you would regret. You'd have regretted it then and you'll regret it now."

"You aren't a man of your word?" It was a low blow at his character. But she was probably the only person her age who was a virgin and didn't want to be. Did she want to coerce Griffin into sleeping with her? Of course not. But she wanted some answers. Was she that unappealing?

Griffin rubbed his jaw. "I am a man of my word, but I don't think you want to sleep with me. You want to prove something to Lawrence and Zoya by pretending we have a relationship that rivals theirs."

His accurate assessment stung. She wished she had something in her personal life to be proud of in the present: a relationship, a house, a family, anything. "Forget I said it." She wasn't good at getting what she wanted from men. Maybe she could put that on her resume: the antimanipulator.

"Tell me what happened between you three. It might make you feel better."

Kit sighed and turned up the air conditioning in the car. "We were part of the Locker project. Lawrence worked physical security. He was nice to everyone, and I thought he liked me. He didn't. He was dating one woman, a civilian, and sleeping with Zoya. I didn't know about their relationship, and I asked him to dinner and tried to kiss him. He turned me down flat and I'm sure he told Zoya, because she was different toward me after the incident."

"If you didn't know, you didn't know. You shouldn't feel bad about it," Griffin said. He pulled into the parking lot of the Tech Buy and found a free space.

Kit hit the door with her fist. "It's humiliating. Most people have dating stories to tell that are positive, and the rejections are vague memories. All I have are rejections. I say the wrong things, I pick the wrong men, and I make a fool of myself. I don't seamlessly fit into social groups."

"You and me both."

"Please," Kit said, trying to imagine Griffin receiving the same looks she did when she spoke to a group. Nope, when women looked at Griffin, their eyes grew wider and they posed as if beckoning him to notice them. "How are you socially awkward? I've seen you in enough groups to know you're good with people."

He turned off the car's ignition. "I'm too blunt. I'm too aggressive. I can't commit. I've heard it all."

"At least you've had relationships," Kit said.

Griffin laughed. "Right. Relationships. One significant one eons ago, and the rest have been a mess. I'm away too long and by the time I return, I've missed too much. I can't connect."

He didn't elaborate on what "one significant

one" meant, and she didn't pry. "I never would have guessed," Kit said.

"I'm not complaining. This is the life that I chose. You're not the only one who doesn't understand relationships."

Thirty minutes later, they were leaving Tech Buy with several bags of supplies. She hadn't found the exact brands she preferred. She blamed the local conference for the run on the more cutting-edge equipment. What she had purchased would have to do. She could tinker with the items, maybe speed them up or change them somewhat, but time was limited and hardware wasn't her expertise.

When they arrived back at the hotel and were in their room, Kit unpacked her devices. She would configure them before she met with Lawrence and Zoya again that evening.

Griffin knelt next to her at the coffee table where she was working. "You look absolutely enraged."

She was focused. Others had commented on her intense look when she worked. "I'm in a bad mood. Ignore it. It will go away."

"I don't want to ignore you. I want you to be in a good place."

Her frame of mind wouldn't stop her from doing what she needed to do. "I'll use Zoya's lead and hack Incognito's version of the Locker to find out what they have in their possession."

"It's not just that I'm concerned about. I'm in charge of your well-being."

Kit turned the new tablet over in her hand. "I

sound like a teenager saying this, but what is wrong with me?"

Griffin touched her cheek. "Nothing is wrong with you."

Griffin had said he had relationship issues, too, but hers went far deeper. "Don't spare my feelings. I need someone to tell me. What will I tell a boyfriend to explain it?"

"To explain what?"

That she was a twenty-eight-year-old virgin. "I haven't had sex."

"That was really your first kiss?" he asked, pulling his hand away.

The withdrawal of his hand was like a slap. "Yes." No point in dancing around it.

"Tell me about having online sex."

She blinked at him. "Are you making fun of me?" In her current state, more emotional abuse would kill her. She'd need a week with a case of lemon-lime soda and ten pounds of jelly beans to recover.

"I'm trying to understand how your mind works."

She'd only had cybersex with Swift. Her experience was limited, even if she'd tried to learn everything she could. "We talk about what we'd like to do with each other if we were in the same room. Like I might tell him what I'm wearing." She looked down at her clothes. "And tell him that I want him to take my clothes off and carry me to the bed. He would cover me with his body." Her mouth went dry, and instead of rehashing a conversation she'd had with

Swift, she was thinking about Griffin and what she wanted from him.

"You're bigger than me, so I'm underneath you and I feel safe. I smell you, the scent of your skin, masculine and clean, and it makes me wish you would hurry. But you want to take your time." Griffin's eyes were riveted on her. "You kiss me softly, and I run my nails down your back. I want it harder. You're more and more excited. You show me with your mouth what you want to do with your lower body." She closed her eyes because looking at him when she was speaking was too intense. "I know that you'll be a big man, so I open my thighs wide, wider, splayed open completely so you can push inside me. When you position yourself, I wiggle to encourage you, but you lift your hips, keeping me from what I most want." She opened her eyes and met his gaze. "You're looking into my eyes, and the connection is right, and I'm hot and wet and ready.

"Holding yourself over me, you move. It takes several thrusts to fit all the way inside because I'm so tight and excited, but I'm wet, and soon I'm begging for more. You move hard and you're so big it hurts, but it hurts so good. The sensations are too much, and you bend to kiss me again. I'm lost to you. I tremble in your arms and you finish inside me, spurting me with heat."

Griffin had stood from her work table, and his hips were in her line of sight. Her words had enticed him. She could see the evidence. Turned on by her story, she touched the front of his pants, running her finger down along the hard ridge that pressed against the fabric.

He didn't stop her. Last night, he had forcefully rejected her. Today was different. She wasn't drugged. Earlier in the day, they'd shared two steamy, shockingly rattling kisses.

Feeling bolder, she stood and stroked her hand down the side of his face, brushing his jawline, tracing his lips with her thumb. She had never touched a man this masculine and hard. She slid her hand around the back of his neck and brought his mouth to hers.

She kissed him, slow and deep. His lips were the only soft part of him. Everything else about Griffin was hard and chiseled from the outside in.

It was their first kiss alone in a room with a bed. She recalled kissing him the night before. He'd turned his mouth away. Not now. He was bent over, his hands at her waist, holding her against his length.

She moved up and down, rubbing against him. She wanted a better angle, a different direction. She pushed his shoulders, shoving him into the wooden chair opposite where she'd been sitting. He didn't stop her and he could have. Easily. He was bigger and stronger than she was, but at this moment, she was in charge. He was hers to command.

She sat on his lap, straddling him. Holding his shoulders, she moved her hips. Her body ached for her to move faster, to find some release for the growing tension. The fabric between them was frustrating. Would he allow her to remove their clothes? She reached for the hem of his shirt and pulled it over his head, tossing it to the floor.

Broad shoulders, defined pectorals, rippling abdominals and pumped biceps. His body was meant to please a woman.

"Looking at you turns me on. How are you this sexy?" she asked. She kissed him again and pressed her body against his bare skin. A shiver of fear coursed through her. For so long, sex had been an unattainable goal. She should have sex for the first time with someone she was in love with and who loved her. She'd just met Griffin. Would she sleep with him, knowing it was nothing to him and would mean so much to her?

He broke the kiss. "Tell me what you're thinking."

"I'm thinking about what's going to happen."

"Do you want to stop?" he asked.

She shook her head. But she was afraid for this to move forward.

Griffin lifted her and set her on the coffee table. He flipped up her skirt and kissed the inside of her thigh. "I don't want this to be about me. I want to relax you. We'll see how many times I can make you come with just my mouth and my hands."

She felt his words at her core. If she wasn't ready before, his words sent a rush of heat over her body. Griffin shifted between her legs and she grabbed the back of his hair, stopping him.

He stilled, lifting his eyes. "What's wrong?"

"I'm scared." She was embarrassed speaking the words, but now that she was standing on the threshold of what she wanted, she felt pressure that it be right and amazing. What if she didn't know what she was doing? What was she supposed to say?

"Tell me why you're scared."

"You won't like it."

He glanced between her legs. "Trust me when I tell you I'll like it."

She swallowed hard. "What if you don't? What if I don't?"

"Then we'll stop. Do you want to stop now?"

She was hot for him. Unreasonably hot, but she found herself nodding. It had moved too fast and while she could have been swept away by Griffin's touch, she wasn't ready.

He helped her off the table. The moment was lost. She had gone so far and then had fled.

"I'll finish this," she said and pointed to her devices.

"Just give me a minute." He went into the bathroom and shut the door.

Kit was left alone with her depressing thoughts, wishing she hadn't stopped Griffin and wishing he could give her more.

Chapter 8

When Griffin had studied this assignment, he hadn't considered it would be a test of his control and of his ability not to sleep with his client.

Kit was a smart and sensual woman, her innocence and sexuality two extremes.

He was turned on. Fiercely. He needed to relieve some of it or he would lose his mind. His thoughts were centered on getting Kit into bed, and they needed to be on keeping her safe.

He climbed into the shower and took himself in hand. He thought of sinking into Kit's body, of laying her on the nearest flat surface.

There was a tap on the door and then it opened. He let go of himself and shut off the water, reaching for a towel. "Are you okay?"

She stood by the sink. "I felt bad about what I did." She glanced at the towel tented across his hips. "Oh, right. I wondered."

He couldn't take more of this. He had to set boundaries. "Kit, I am fine with us not having sex and I will keep my hands off you, but no more talk of sex. No more kissing. No touching each other."

"Are you mad?"

Not mad. His blood was pulsing with lust. "No."

"You sound mad."

This was where her inexperience with men showed. "Kit, I'm turned on and I'm controlling it. If you sense tension, the tension is my body wanting to finish."

She licked her lips, her pink tongue drawing his attention. "I want to try again."

He shook his head. "No."

"I had an idea of what my first time would be like."

"I'm not taking your virginity, and that's not under discussion."

She looked again at the front of his towel. "I can leave you to finish, then."

The disappointment was so heavy in her voice, he almost relented. But if he slept with her, or kissed her, or engaged in any type of sex with her, it would impact their relationship and the mission. Based on her reaction to him kissing her thigh, she wasn't ready for more with a man. While sex relaxed him, it might upset her.

He wouldn't touch her again. He could get through this mission and focus.

* * *

Griffin carried the repurposed costume box to Lawrence and Zoya's room. It was filled with Kit's computer equipment. She was behind him. Since their almost-sex earlier, she was avoiding eye contact and had returned to her former quiet self.

He didn't like it. He wasn't big on talking about feelings, and she wasn't, either. He wanted to clear the air, but what could he say that wouldn't make this worse?

He set the box on the floor and had her stand next to it, away from the door. Since they'd been greeted with the muzzle of a gun earlier, he wasn't taking chances.

Zoya opened the door wearing a silk robe parted to reveal cleavage. Were they interrupting Lawrence and Zoya? They'd known he and Kit were coming.

She opened the door wide and tucked a long strand of hair behind her ear. "Come in."

Over her shoulder, Lawrence was seated at a long table against the window wearing clothes. No rumpled sheets or the scent of sex and sweat in the air. Maybe Zoya just liked to dress in next-to-nothing and flaunt her body.

Griffin nodded to Kit that it was safe, and she entered the room. Griffin checked under the beds, the bathroom and the closets. All were empty.

Lawrence seemed amused. "FBI?"

Griffin shook his head. Whom he worked for wasn't important. The West Company was notorious, but little was known about them, and that was how the company liked it. Their missions and operations were whispered about as if they were urban legends.

Kit sat on the end of the table and started setting up her equipment. "How did you find Incognito's partial version of the Locker? Do you know how much of it they have?"

Lawrence watched her work. "We've been tracking it. Zoya handled the networking part of the project. We think they have about seventy-five percent of it."

Kit nodded. "Did you leave a back door to get inside when we were working on the project?"

Zoya shook her head. "I tried to. Someone found it and sealed it off. We're working blind, but I know what I'm looking for. When the Locker is running at full capacity, it creates a fair amount of traffic to and from the major hubs. Unless Incognito hacked it and then changed the code or redirected network activity, I sniff out the location by traffic content. They have the IP changing every three to seventeen minutes, but I know the MAC address of the device hosting the incomplete copy."

Kit seemed to understand what Zoya was saying. Griffin was lost.

"How long have you been together?" Lawrence asked.

Griffin and Kit hadn't discussed their cover with Lawrence and Zoya. Would Kit tell them the truth? He let her field the question.

"We've been lovers for a few months," Kit said.

Lawrence appeared surprised, and Zoya narrowed

her eyes. "You two are a couple? I thought you were partners. Working partners."

"We're that, too," Griffin said.

Kit had her reasons for telling them she and Griffin were together, and he didn't counter her words. Keeping a consistent cover was easier. Less to remember and less likely they'd be caught in a lie.

Kit positioned her tablet on the table. "You're sure about this information?"

Lawrence nodded. "Zoya's the best. We've checked our numbers. We have a location."

Kit drummed her fingers against the table. "The Locker should be harder to find. It should disguise its traffic."

"We have the location of the copy. It didn't have the same traffic rerouting algorithms or firewalls," Zoya said. "Incognito must have tried to rebuild the parts they haven't stolen, but they haven't achieved the same caliber protection methods."

"I can try to access the copy and destroy whatever parts I can in the time I have," Kit said. "I'll have about fifteen seconds before I'm detected and tossed out."

"Fifteen seconds is generous," Zoya said.

"It's also assuming I don't get caught in the honey pot, they haven't modified the code to sever my connection immediately, and they haven't added levels of authentication." Kit took a deep breath. "I'll need you to keep my IP moving, okay?"

Zoya sat, gathered her hair in her hand and secured

it on top her head with a clip from her robe. "I can do that. You ready?"

Lawrence took a few steps away from the table and stood next to Griffin. "They're incredible."

"Talented," Griffin said. Of course they were. Zoya was confident. Kit seemed nervous.

Kit stopped typing, her hands hovering above the keys, and looked at Griffin. "Before we do this, could I talk to you alone?"

He nodded. She gestured to the bathroom, and he followed her in. She shut the door, turned on the fan and ran the water.

"Are you attracted to me or is a woman like Zoya more your speed? Or someone like my sister?"

This wasn't the time or place to have this conversation. "You want to talk about this now?" Griffin asked.

"I'm upset, and that question is rattling around in my brain. When I'm upset I can't think clearly. I can't afford to make mistakes. Fifteen seconds isn't a lot of time to launch an e-missile, direct it into the guts of the code and destroy it."

"However I answer your question will cause a problem."

She sighed. "Play it straight with me."

"You are not the type of woman I usually date."

Her shoulders sagged, and she looked at the floor.

"But," he said, lifting her chin to look at him, "I think you are beautiful and smart and charming. I like spending time with you. I wouldn't have accepted this assignment if I didn't enjoy being with you. I'm attracted to you, but you are not ready for us to explore that attraction, and I'm not prepared to risk another distraction."

She ran her finger down his body. She seemed to enjoy touching him. If she were a more experienced woman under different circumstances, he would have let her take off his clothes and do whatever she wanted to him, as long as he could do the same to her.

"That makes me feel better," Kit said.

"We can talk about this later," Griffin said. "Are you ready?" he asked and gestured toward the door.

They exited the bathroom. Zoya smirked. "Needed a quickie for stress release?"

Kit said nothing and took her seat. "I'm ready to go. Tell me when."

Zoya started typing. "Now. Go now."

Fifteen seconds. Kit focused on what she knew about the Locker and not on the doubts that pounded at her or the clock ticking.

She hadn't built the entire system. She'd worked on a small part of the Locker. She could encounter pieces she hadn't been aware of and be unable to circumvent them. If Incognito had possessed the Locker for any period of time, they could have made changes.

It took her eight seconds to breach the firewall and two more to figure out she'd been led into a trap.

"It's not real. It's a honey pot." She disconnected her computer, but she'd been detected and it was too late.

"Can't be. I'm sure it is the real deal," Zoya said.

"Did you mask my network traffic?" Kit asked.

Zoya nodded. "Yes. I think so."

Kit pulled cords from the devices. "Thinking is not enough." Kit's anxiety twisted her stomach into knots. "We have to get out of this room. Burn these computers and this equipment. They're tainted."

She tore the electrical cords from the wall and popped out the batteries on the devices.

Griffin was at her side. "How do you know you were caught?"

"No time to explain." She threw the devices into the box. If anyone else used them, they could be targeted by Incognito. "They're close. They know."

Griffin didn't question her further. "To the car. Immediately."

They started for the door, but Lawrence and Zoya stopped to pack.

"There's no time," Kit said. Incognito had set a trap to target anyone looking for the Locker, including the government. The firewalls Kit had set up to protect her computer weren't impenetrable, and Zoya's network address masking could have been stripped away.

Zoya was shoving items in her suitcase. "You're being a hysteric. No one can figure out where we are and get here that quickly."

"Unless they are already at the conference," Kit said, thinking of the drugging at the rave last night. Incognito might already be looking for her, and they might already suspect she was at Gamer Con. They knew her identity and they had stalked her to her sister's birthday party. They were closing in on her.

Lawrence took Zoya's hand. "I will replace anything we lose. I cannot replace your life."

Zoya let out a grunt of frustration, but she stopped packing.

They ran for the elevators. The lights in the hotel went out, and the elevator doors closed. Turning off the power was one of Incognito's signature moves. It was a show of their strength and abilities. Without the light from the windows at the far ends of the hallway, they would have been surrounded in pitch-blackness.

They had no choice but to use the stairwell. Racing down the stairs, taking them several at a time, they made it to the lobby. It was crowded. Security for the convention was in place around the room, and some guests were complaining about the electricity, but no one seemed panicked. After about thirty minutes when the Nevada sun baked the hotel and the restaurants were unable to cook and serve food, the anger would boil over.

A blackout could be explained by a power surge or a problem at the electric company, but this was Incognito.

No one was running or searching for them. Maybe they'd been lucky and Incognito hadn't tracked her that quickly. Kit had made a colossal mistake trusting that Zoya knew what she was doing. Kit should have validated and reviewed Zoya's intel first. Zoya was good. Incognito was better.

Griffin didn't slow down. Kit stayed close to him. He was armed and carrying the box of equipment under his arm. "Parking garage," he said.

They raced down the hallway toward the garage. Kit opened the metal door leading out of the hotel and the heat hit her, almost sucking the air from her lungs.

Inside the parking structure, they heard only the occasional car horn, squealing tires and engines. A car drove toward them and Kit's heart seized. The driver ignored them. Not Incognito.

Zoya and Lawrence were arguing in French. Kit wasn't fluent and only understood every few words. Lawrence was blaming Zoya for this and Zoya blamed Kit.

Kit blamed all three of them. Griffin had tried to warn her. She should have listened to him.

They took the stairs to the level where Griffin was parked and ran for his car.

When they reached the car, relief washed over her. They were getting away! They could find another place, a safer place, regroup and try again. Hope built in Kit's chest. They had outmaneuvered Incognito. She felt like she had run a marathon and the finish line was in sight.

Gunfire exploded around them.

Griffin dropped the box and pushed Kit around a concrete pillar next to the car. "Stay here. Stay down." Griffin withdrew his gun and peered around the pillar, returning fire. "They're using the cars for cover. I can't get a clean shot."

Incognito could have staked out the entire hotel, knowing they'd appear. Lawrence and Zoya were squatting behind a car. How would they get out of this?

The gunfire stopped.

A voice came from between the cars. "Lawrence, if you hand them over, we won't have trouble."

Alarm skittered through Kit. Had Lawrence sold them out?

"My wife's been hit. She's bleeding," Lawrence said.

Panic flared, making Kit's stomach twist. Zoya was hurt. She needed medical care, and they were pinned down in the parking structure.

"If you turn yourself in to us, we'll see she has the medical care she needs," said the voice from between the cars.

Kit glanced at Zoya and Lawrence. Griffin's hand was gripping her arm, not letting her move from their position. Zoya was holding her shoulder, and her robe was red with blood.

Lawrence held a gun at her and Griffin. He glanced at his wife. "We need to go with them and they'll heal her. Please, do it for Zoya." He sounded anguished.

"You did this?" Zoya asked.

Lawrence ran his hand through his hair. "They needed help. The United States is out of control. They're using the Locker to control every bit of data on the internet. They have to be stopped."

Griffin pointed his gun at Lawrence. "Drop it. We'll get the women out of here. We'll find Zoya medical help. You don't have to turn us over to Incognito."

Lawrence shook his head. "They'll kill me. They'll find me. I agreed to help them. I already took the money."

"If this was your plan, why didn't you call them when we first made contact?" Kit asked. He could have brought them to the hotel room and Kit, Griffin and Zoya would have been trapped inside.

"They wanted to test you to see if you were as good as everyone says. They wanted to see if you could breach their network. They wanted proof you were Lotus," Lawrence said.

Kit had passed their test, and now Incognito had confirmed her identity and wanted her to work for them. Lawrence seemed to think he was doing the right thing, or maybe he had let the money convince him it was the right thing.

"They shot Zoya. You have to know they'll kill you either way," Kit said.

Lawrence's eyes were filled with fear. "We can't escape." He jabbed a hand through his hair.

Zoya moaned. "Find Arsenic." She sounded tired and winded.

Kit wasn't sure she had heard her correctly. "Arsenic isn't well."

One of the first engineers on the Locker had recruited the computer scientists and engineers who had worked on the project. Arsenic had suffered a massive stroke and had been hospitalized. He hadn't recovered and couldn't talk or walk. He was in a vegetative state, a shell of the genius he once was.

Zoya's eyes were glossy. "Find him."

"Arsenic is out there?" Lawrence asked, sounding bewildered.

"Yes," Zoya said.

Kit tried to process that and couldn't. Was Zoya losing blood and hallucinating? "Where should I look for him?"

Zoya said nothing.

"You betrayed me, Zoya. You kept secrets. Your secret world on that blasted computer. You never let me inside," Lawrence said. His hands were shaking, and sweat dripped down his face.

Lawrence lowered his gun and shot Zoya. Lawrence turned his gun on himself. Another shot and Lawrence fell to the ground next to his wife. Kit screamed and turned away.

"I count two shots. That means two of you are alive." The voice from between the cars again, cold and gruff.

Griffin pressed a finger over his lips. He would get them out of this. Kit couldn't look at Lawrence or Zoya. Why had Lawrence chosen that way out? They could have escaped.

Griffin knelt on the ground and aimed his gun. He fired. A yelp from someone; he had hit his target.

"Run!" Griffin said.

They dashed from the concrete pillar, and Griffin grabbed her arm and pointed to a black car. "Get in."

It was locked. Griffin broke the driver's side window with his elbow, opened the door and hit the unlock button. Kit climbed inside. Griffin tore off the steering panel. Kit heard footsteps and turned around. She didn't see anyone. Where were they? She felt them coming. Terror gripped her, making words impossible.

Griffin connected two wires. The car started.

He backed out of the spot, narrowly missing the cars parked behind them.

"Are we being followed?" Griffin asked.

She twisted in her seat to look behind them. She didn't see anyone in pursuit.

"If Incognito has men posted everywhere, we might have been dealing with that one attacker," Griffin said. "The other posts might not have assembled as backup in time."

Driving the wrong way down a one-way lane, Griffin skidded the car out of the parking garage. They hit the street and Griffin didn't slow down.

Griffin alerted Connor they had two bodies in the garage and possible Incognito assassins waiting at the conference center and hotel, looking for them.

When he disconnected his call, he turned to Kit. They had been driving for ten minutes and he hadn't spotted a tail. He didn't know their next move. Kit had been silent. "Are you okay?" he asked.

Kit was pale but calm. "Lawrence shot Zoya and killed himself."

They had witnessed a deeply disturbing incident. She wasn't accustomed to violence and death. "Yes."

"I don't understand it."

"He was in over his head and he wanted a way out. If Incognito had caught him, they would have killed him." Or tortured him and then killed him. "If they didn't, the United States would have thrown him in jail." Traitors never fared well, and Griffin had no sympathy for the man who had sold out Kit and Zoya. Griffin wanted to distract Kit and take her mind off the deaths of her two associates. "Tell me what Zoya meant about Arsenic."

"Arsenic was amazing with a computer before his stroke. In the middle of the Locker project, he was hospitalized, and he didn't return."

Sounded shady, like someone was hiding something. "What else do you know about him?" Griffin asked.

"He's an off-the-charts genius, but he's quirky. Probably some undiagnosed form of autism. He was a lead designer on the Locker. He had a hand in selecting every member of the team."

"Where is he now?" Griffin asked.

"The last I heard, he was recovering in a medical facility in Maryland. His mother lives in the area."

"What's the name of the facility?"

"Morningside Acres in Bel Air."

"I'll call Connor. We're headed there."

Kit touched his arm. "If Zoya suspected that Arsenic was alive, Incognito would know it, too."

He hoped not. Lawrence had seemed surprised by the information. "Maybe not. Do you know Arsenic's real name?"

"No real names were to be exchanged. It was part of the security around the project. But it happened," Kit said.

"We'll get his real name and check the patient records at the facility where he's staying."

Forty minutes later, Kate West had sent a list of

possible names for Arsenic. By looking at patient admission dates, they believed John Conrad was Arsenic, mastermind behind the Locker. John Conrad had a thin trail of records prior to being enrolled at Morningside, giving away that John Conrad was likely a government-issued identity.

"He was completely gone," Kit said. "Even if he's there and knows who I am, he couldn't speak to me."

"Zoya directed us to find him. We need to follow her lead. It's the only one we have."

"A lead or a trap?" Kat asked.

"Could be either. But I'm prepared to handle both."

After some sleep, a military flight and an hour in their rental car, Griffin and Kit were pulling into the campus of the Morningside Acres Rehabilitation Center located in the suburbs of Bel Air in Maryland. The road leading to the main facility was lined with purple and yellow flowers, and the green grass surrounding the property looked like it was manicured with scissors.

Based on his medical insurance claims, John Conrad was in-house. A call to the front desk, and Griffin was informed Mr. Conrad could have visitors. If she and Griffin could walk in, so could Incognito. If they hadn't already approached him, they must not have connected Arsenic to John Conrad, or Arsenic was too far gone to be of use to them. Whoever Arsenic/John Conrad had been before working on the Locker had been scrubbed from official government records.

How had Zoya known so much about Arsenic?

Griffin parked their rental car and walked to the visitor's entrance.

Griffin took her hand in his. "Are you feeling okay?"

"Haven't slept enough and I'm hungry, but I'm fine." She was high-strung, thinking about Arsenic, Lawrence and Zoya. She couldn't sleep well.

Griffin looked apologetic. "I forgot about food. We'll eat soon."

An orderly pushed a man in a wheelchair into the patient visiting area. Though his eyes were open, the man didn't move his head to acknowledge her. No flash of recognition in his eyes. He was frail and still.

He wasn't Arsenic. Even considering the hard years of living in a rehab facility poststroke, this wasn't him. "This is John Conrad?" she asked the orderly.

The orderly nodded. "I've been taking care of Mr. Conrad since he arrived. He doesn't get many visitors. I was happy to hear some old friends were coming to see him. I will be honest with you, though. He doesn't recognize many people, so please don't be hurt if he doesn't know who you are."

Kit faced Griffin and shook her head. "It's not him. We've made a mistake. This is the wrong man."

The orderly frowned.

Griffin's mouth drew into a hard line. "We're sorry to have wasted your time." He guided Kit out of the building.

"I don't understand this," Kit said. "Zoya said Arsenic is alive, but that was not him."

"Are you sure? Do you want to look again?" Griffin asked.

Kit shook her head. "It wasn't him. I'm certain of it. What now? Where do we go from here?"

"If he's the wrong man, then the right man is out there somewhere, and we have to find him before Incognito does."

Kit hated sleeping in hotel rooms. She missed her bed and her family. She missed her routine. The one comfort was the sound of the water from the Chesapeake Bay lapping against the shore. They were only a few hundred feet from the waterline.

Griffin had gone to buy food. He'd wanted her to go with him, but she needed time alone. She'd promised to keep the door locked and not open it for anyone.

Arsenic was somewhere in the world. Was he willingly working with Incognito? Kit hadn't stayed in touch with anyone from the Locker project. It had seemed safer, and she had been advised not to.

Kit trudged to the bathroom to brush her teeth before bed. She stumbled and fell against the doorjamb, catching herself with her hands. When she righted herself and looked in the mirror, she saw a familiar face. Turning slowly, her heart hammering hard, she met his ice-cold gaze.

Arsenic.

Chapter 9

Nothing in those eyes was vacant. Arsenic was the same as she had remembered. Too thin, tall, with sharp eyes and a beak-shaped nose that reminded her of a hawk.

He aimed a gun at her head. "Why are you looking for me? What do you want?"

How had he known? "It's me, Kit Walker. Lotus. Zoya told me to find you." Kit could say this without selling Zoya out, since she was dead.

"I know who you are. Where is Zoya?" he asked.

Sadness tightened her throat. "Dead."

"You're lying!" His voice lacked conviction.

She wished she was. "Incognito is hunting us. Killing or capturing everyone who's worked on the Locker. Incognito followed us to Gamer Con. Zoya's husband sold us out. He planned to hand us over to Incognito but ended up killing himself and her."

Arsenic's eyes narrowed. "I told her not to go to Gamer Con."

What was the relationship between Arsenic and Zoya? He spoke of her with a closeness and softness in his voice.

"I'm sorry for your loss. It was truly awful," Kit said.

"How did you escape them? Did they follow you?"

Arsenic's arms were lifted above his head, and the gun clattered to the floor. Griffin had moved so quietly, Kit hadn't heard him enter the hotel room. Griffin shoved Arsenic into the dresser.

Griffin held the gun on Arsenic. "Who are you?"

Kit stepped in front of Griffin, causing him to lower his gun. "Griffin, stop. This is Arsenic. He's scared, too. He's here to find out why we're looking for him." Though he had broken into her hotel room and pointed a gun at her, she sensed he wasn't planning to harm her. He wanted to protect himself.

Griffin grabbed Arsenic and hauled him to his feet. "Talk fast."

"You came looking for me. I needed to know why," Arsenic said.

Griffin released Arsenic but didn't take his eyes off him.

Arsenic laughed, a sick, maniacal laugh. "Building the Locker was a mistake. I shouldn't have signed on for the project. I should never have let anyone have it. It's too strong. It can be used for the wrong reasons."

"It's protected the United States' networks for years," Kit said carefully. Lawrence had implied the US was using it for nefarious purposes. Kit wasn't naive, but she believed that the work she had done had been in support of a country she loved. Had she been wrong to believe it was being used for good?

"It does those things, but once it's been compromised, it's a failure. A six-hundred-million-dollar failure. Every day some young hotshot comes up the ranks and learns a new way to break into systems. Ways you and I never thought of and using technology that didn't exist five years ago. How can anything protect itself against that?" Arsenic asked.

"Will you help us counter Incognito's attempt to gain full control of the Locker?" Kit asked.

Arsenic shook his head. "I don't want to get involved with another Locker. It was hard enough to get out the first time."

Kit tried to keep up, but she was missing an important part of the story. "How did you get out? We were told you had a stroke."

"Months of planning and many allies. I tried to pull Zoya out, too, but she refused. She had already fallen for Lawrence and declined to leave the project and go underground with me."

Kit heard the grief in his voice. "I didn't realize you and Zoya were so close."

"She's my daughter."

Surprise rolled over her. She hadn't before made the connection. A fresh round of grief struck her thinking of how Arsenic must feel to learn about his daughter's death in this way.

Arsenic took a tissue from the box on the dresser and blotted his bleeding nose. "A friend at the in-patient clinic calls me when someone shows up to visit me. Can't be too careful."

"How have you stayed hidden?" Kit asked.

"I waited until someone fitting my general description was admitted to the hospital. Then I gave him my government-issued new identity that I was supposed to use when I finished the project. I forged a fresh one for myself, one the government was unaware of."

A simple matter for someone like Arsenic. He was smart and well-connected. "If we find and stop Incognito, then the threat against you will be eliminated."

"One quality that I liked about you, and one of the reasons I picked you for the project, is that you're naive. Your innocence is refreshing. There are no good guys or bad guys, just people who have an agenda. Stopping Incognito won't mean that I can live my life on the grid. Someone will always want a piece of me."

But not everyone was willing to resort to violence and kidnapping to meet their objectives. "If Incognito uses the Locker against us, they'll have access to the United States' classified intel. They'll know names of undercover operatives and mission secrets."

Arsenic shrugged. "So what?"

"If covers are blown and information made public, agents and operatives will be killed," Kit said.

"That's a risk every operative for the United States

knows," Arsenic said. "I'll make a deal with you. Don't blow my cover. As far as Uncle Sam knows, I'm incapacitated and won't recover. Don't follow me. Don't alert anyone that I'm alive. If you grant me this favor, I'll consider helping you."

"Consider helping us?" Kit asked.

Arsenic's face was unreadable. "I'll be in touch when I've made a decision."

Kit exchanged glances with Griffin.

"If that's the best you're offering, then fine. We'll keep your secret," Griffin said.

Arsenic nodded once and left their hotel room.

"What do you make of that?" Griffin asked.

"He is a little peculiar," Kit said. "But I think he'll help us. I think he'll do the right thing."

"We need to head back to California," Griffin said.

"No rest for the weary?" Kit asked, already knowing the answer.

"You can sleep on my shoulder on the flight."

Sleeping on his shoulder was like sleeping on a rock. "Not as comfortable as you might think."

"You can lie across my lap," he said.

That had interesting possibilities. "Could we sleep here tonight?"

"If Arsenic knew we were here, then someone else might know," Griffin said.

Kit took a deep breath. Another plane flight. "Can I at least negotiate for a coffee?"

Griffin preferred spending the night in a safe house more than he liked a hotel room, and as safe houses went, this one wasn't bad. Arsenic's appearance was a testament to why they were safer under the radar. Griffin had used a fake identity provided to him by the West Company to check into the hotel room in Maryland, but Griffin would not underestimate Incognito.

Griffin watched Kit pushing food around her plate.

It had been a long flight and he was tired, but until she slept, he wouldn't either.

"Two more people died. How many more will because of this project?" Kit asked. Reality was catching up with her.

"As many as Incognito kills until we stop them," Griffin said. Which could be dozens. Incognito had come too far and had proven nothing would slow them down.

Kit circled the small wood table and pushed it away from him. She sat in his lap and laid her head on his shoulder. "Hold me. Please."

He rested his arms against her waist. Hugs were okay. She didn't have anyone else to confide in, no one else whom she could talk with about what had happened. This was a friendship hug. Griffin liked the scent of her hair, and her body pressed to his felt good. He wouldn't let this morph in to anything else. "The woman who prefers the computer above all else is asking for human contact?"

Kit kissed the tip of his ear. "I could have been killed today. I could be killed tomorrow. I suppose that's always been true, but with assassins gunning for me, the probability is higher than random chance."

She had her arm around his shoulders, and the other hand stroked his face. Comfort and friendship were shifting into decidedly sexual territory. It happened when they were alone and when she touched him. Heat scorched him. Sleeping with her was off the table, and everything leading to that point had scared her.

He had to keep control. Did she know what she was doing?

She shifted then, moving astride him. She rocked her hips into his.

She knew exactly what she was doing.

"You look so hot in jeans and a T-shirt," she said. "I need to feel your skin against mine."

He went hard at the idea and shifted his hips away. "You don't know what you're saying." He set his hands on the seat of his chair. He could not reach for her again, not in friendship or for any other reason. His control would snap and he would have sex with her. She had asked him to. She had done things to imply she wanted him and her current position left little to the imagination. But he couldn't. Her virginity was a red flag waving back and forth, warning him to keep away. Leaving her untouched was another objective he had added to the mission.

"I get hot just looking at you," she said.

His body hardened to a painful degree, and his brain shifted into full-on lust. Desire clamored at him to strip them naked. Logic slowed him down. He couldn't sleep with her. His mission was to protect her. His doubts about his ability to do that pressed on him. He had managed so far, but how much of that was luck?

Sleeping with a man for the first time was an experience she should have with someone special, someone who would treasure the memory, love her and give everything a woman like her deserved the first time: flowers, promises and romance.

In the safe house, they had two borderline uncomfortable beds, no wine and no champagne, and no love between them.

"Tell me what you like," she said, reaching between them and rubbing the front of his jeans. They had been down this path before. If he let her continue, she would stop. She would become nervous, and he wouldn't have to do anything. He'd let her burn herself out.

In his current state, he wanted nothing more than to get her on her back and pound into her until she was chanting his name. Instead, he would keep his hands on the chair. She could say whatever she wanted and he would play this game, but he would not touch her.

"I like what you're doing," he said.

She shivered. "What about your favorite position? Do you like a woman on top? Or do you like being in control?"

"I would ask you that question, because every position feels good to me, but you don't know what you like," he said.

"You could help me figure it out," she said. She

licked her bottom lip. "I'm a big fan of experimentation."

A little further and she would freak out and stop. This wasn't how she'd want her first time. "How do you want me to do you first? Against the wall with your legs around my waist? Or on the bed, on your hands and knees, being slammed into from behind?" he asked. He meant the words to be crude because to imply that sex between them would be anything more than a physical act was wrong.

Her eyes grew wider and he waited. Any moment now, she would stop.

"Whatever you want to do, I want you to do it hard." She reached into his pants and he went almost mindless.

She wasn't backing down, and he was past the point where he could stop this. He removed his shirt, knowing she liked him bare-chested.

She smiled and ran one hand over his chest, her other hand still in his pants, stroking him. "Hard and hot." She kissed his skin, running her mouth across every inch and then skating lower until she was face-to-face with his arousal.

She unbuttoned and unzipped his pants and then pulled him free.

Now she would back off. No way was this happening.

She looked at him and traced his length with her fingertip. She sucked in her breath. A woman had never looked at him this way, thinking, pining for it.

"Kit, consider what you're doing."

"I don't know what I'm doing. I haven't done this. But I think you'll let me try."

Some men might find an experienced woman sexier, but the awe in Kit's face and the wonder in her eyes was enough to send him over the edge.

She stuck out her tongue and licked his tip. His right hand left the chair and forked into her hair. She hollowed her cheeks, sucking just the tip, and his body bucked involuntarily. He worked to keep himself pinned to the seat. Then she put him further into her mouth. He let out his breath in a hiss.

The heat and suction of her mouth were incredible. She wrapped her hands around the base, and her mouth and hands moved in sequence.

He should have stopped her long before now, but her bobbing head and the sensation rolling over him made that impossible.

Then she lifted her eyes and met his gaze. He went off. Realizing it might be too much for her, he pulled her away. She had a look of shock and excitement on her face.

"I did it," she said. "Did you like it?"

What could he say to her? She seemed vulnerable, anxious for praise, and he wanted to find the right words. "It was phenomenal. Great technique."

"I'll have to try that again."

Possessiveness hit him like a knife to the stomach. He pulled her against him. "You will not do that with another man. Not while we are together."

Kit touched the corner of her mouth. "Then you and I will do that again."

"Will you let me do the same to you?"

He reached into her pants, slipping his hand over her panties, and found her wet, almost dripping through the silky cloth. "You want more. You want me."

He wanted to push his fingers inside her and give her a series of orgasms that would leave her dizzy, but knowing he was the first man to do this with her, he wanted it to be tender, as well.

"I told you I wanted you." She sounded breathless, and her cheeks were flushed with excitement.

Promising himself this wouldn't escalate into intercourse, he stood, swept her into his arms, and laid her on the narrow bed.

"Is this okay?" he asked, needing to know she hadn't changed her mind.

She touched his hair, softly, combing her fingers through it. "It's okay. I'll tell you if it's not."

He pulled her shirt over her head and brought his hands to her breasts. He squeezed them together, perfect handfuls, and lowered the fabric covering them. He kissed the pert tips, sucking them into his mouth and enjoying the sounds she made. She arched under his touch.

Massaging her breasts with his right hand, he slid his left hand lower to the top of her pants. He shimmied them down her thighs, and she kicked them off.

"Tell me if I do anything you don't like." Hooking his thumbs in the sides of her panties, he pulled them off and tossed them out of the way.

She unsnapped her bra, and it joined her clothes

on the floor. She was absolutely bare before him, and he took a moment to drink in her beauty.

His pants had to stay on. They were unzipped, but he needed the physical barrier. He could too easily forget, climb on top of her, and shove inside her. Lust was making him forget the rules.

He reached between her legs, but she was holding her knees together. He parted her thighs with a nudge of his hand. "Open for me."

She did and he moved her legs further, spreading her feet to the edges of the bed. He blew across her and then slid a finger inside her. She grabbed his hand and gasped.

"That feels so good," she said.

He moved his finger in and out and then added another. Two fingers were enough. He could try for three, but it might hurt her. "You are so tight."

"Griffin, I need you to hold me."

He'd give her whatever she needed. The preciousness of what they were doing wasn't lost on him. She wasn't a relationship-weary operative with dozens of experiences with men.

He shifted to slide next to her, cradling her against him, propping himself on his elbow so he could look at her. Adding his thumb to the motion between her thighs, he moved in small circles, pressing lightly and watching her face to gauge her reaction.

She closed her eyes and lifted her hips, as if seeking more. The bliss written on her face and the soft moans from her throat made it almost too tempting for him to remove his pants and slide inside her.

The fit would be unbelievably tight, but she wanted him. Griffin marshaled his control. He couldn't cross that line with her. They had a professional relationship. They weren't a couple. With his hand inside her, however, this was a contrary thought. Even as he recognized that, he couldn't stop.

She was close to finishing, and he wanted to be the first man to give her an orgasm with his hand. Her breath came in quicker pants and she was pressing hard against his fingers. If they were having sex, this is when she would urge him to move harder and faster, and he would willingly oblige.

She trembled around him, making the most sensual noises, and then stilled, looking at him, astonished.

He removed his fingers from her slowly. She hadn't said anything, and he had the impression he might have done something wrong. He hadn't done this with another woman and had it not lead to sex. He was ready for another round. He ignored the impulse to take this further.

"What are you thinking about?" she asked.

"You. Only you."

She blushed and moved closer to him. "Will you sleep here?"

On a single bed? They'd be pressed together all night, and he liked his space. It would be uncomfortable. He felt the word *no* on his tongue, but decided against denying her. A little discomfort to please her was worth it.

* * *

Kit couldn't sleep. Griffin was behind her, his heavy arm around her, his breath light in her hair.

She wanted to have sex with him again. She wanted him to work that same magic with his hands. But she didn't know how to ask him. She pressed her rear end against him and his hand came to her hip. "Sleep."

She wiggled more. "I don't want to sleep."

He growled. "You want sleep. You'll regret it in the morning."

"I know what I will and won't regret. I will not regret anything I do with you."

He groaned. "You're killing me."

In the best way, right? Could she break him down? She was surprised he had allowed their physical relationship to progress as far as it had after so many rejections. "I want to try some things."

"My clothes stay on until you define what things."

"You already took off your shirt," Kit said.

"For you."

"I'm naked," Kit said. She wasn't self-conscious about it, which surprised her. She had never been naked with a man, over the internet or in person.

"I know," he said.

She felt increasingly comfortable telling him what she wanted. "I think we should have sex. We basically already have."

"We have not basically done anything. There are lines."

"We've blurred those lines. Please don't make me beg." She would plead with him to be reasonable or try other methods. She wasn't entirely sure what had changed his mind earlier, but she wanted the key to unlock his attention and affection.

"My intention isn't to make you beg. I want you to go to sleep."

If they were on the computer, she would say something blatantly sexual and see if he took the bait. Would that work in person?

"What's the sexiest outfit you've seen a woman wear?" Why didn't that sound hot?

"Nothing. I prefer a woman wearing nothing."

She was wearing nothing. "You're not a lingerie person?"

Griffin sighed. "Lingerie gets in the way."

Wearing lingerie was out, and he wasn't sounding like he was any more in the mood. She had thought Griffin would be an all-night-long man. Was she wrong? Was it her?

"Can I see your tattoos?" she asked.

"It's dark," he said. He sounded grumpy.

She'd try one more time. "Do you have any sexual fantasies?"

He rose from the bed in one swift motion. She was so close to the edge of it, she almost fell out.

"Kit, I don't know what you are trying to do to me, but I am trying to be a stand-up guy. I'm trying to preserve your virginity so when this is over, you can have an actual relationship with a man who cares about you and have sex for the first time with him and have it be meaningful to both of you."

Questions about what he said ping-ponged through

her head. "What do you mean, 'when this is over'?" She didn't bother trying to hide her hurt. Didn't what they were doing mean anything to him? She wasn't expecting a diamond ring, but was he saying she was nothing to him?

"When I am no longer responsible for you, this will be over," he said.

Responsible for her, like he was her babysitter? "What do you mean by 'actual relationship'?"

"I mean, you should be someone's girlfriend. Be with someone who treats you how you want to be treated." He jammed his hand through his hair and looked away from her. Emotion played across his face briefly before his expression turned stoic.

Kit felt silly. She had assigned meaning to what they had done, but it hadn't meant anything to him. He wasn't a friend, let alone a lover. He wasn't in her life for long. She had intellectually known that, known that he would leave, but she had pictured exchanging texts and staying in touch.

"Why not you?" she asked.

"I don't understand the question." He sounded exhausted, and she wished she had gone to sleep when he had encouraged her to.

"Why aren't you interested in being with me?"

It was hard to see his face with only a dim light on in the room. "It's not about what I'm interested in. I've explained this before."

"Your responsibilities," she said, bitterness rising inside her. Every man she had been interested in had a reason why he couldn't be with her. It was pathetic to line them up, a long list of failures and misunderstandings and embarrassment for her.

"Right, my responsibilities."

He wasn't trying to make her feel better. He didn't care enough to bother to lie. He lay on the empty bed. End of discussion.

The bed was still warm from where he had been. Kit would not cry. It was too quiet and he would hear her. Giving him that power over her was unacceptable.

For the hundredth time since meeting Griffin, Kit wished they had computers between them to communicate. Talking in person hurt more. In person was much harder. That connection felt more real and intense, and yet she wasn't sure if it was genuine at all.

Chapter 10

Griffin didn't take sleeping with Kit lightly. She would grow more attached to him. From the first time he had helped her escape the assassins looking for her, she had clung to him more than she should. He knew the power that he had over her, and he'd abused it. His hands did not belong on her.

The coward's option was to call Connor, explain he couldn't continue to guard her and have someone else assigned to protect her. Doing that would hurt her. She wouldn't understand. She would shut down. What could he do? He'd known letting their relationship escalate would bring trouble, and he'd allowed it.

He slept for several hours and woke to the sound of her crying. It would have hurt less if she had stuck a knife in his back.

He had made her cry. He wasn't an egomaniac. This situation brought a great deal of stress. She had witnessed murders, had been taken from her home and had faced off against cyberfriends who had turned out to be something other than the people she knew online. Her emotions weren't centered on him, but her tears were most definitely about him.

Griffin didn't deal well with crying women. He didn't know how to handle them. Since his wife had died, most of his relationships were in the field, with women who were as career-focused as he was, who were hard around the edges, who were looking to sleep with someone for sport and stress relief, women who didn't invest emotionally in a one-time deal.

"Please, please don't cry," he said.

She sniffed but said nothing.

"Kit, talk to me."

"What do you want me to say?" she asked, anger sharp in her tone.

What did he want her to say? Tell him she was fine and give him the salve he needed for his guilt? She felt how she did because of his actions. He had to take responsibility for that. "Tell me what I can do to make this right." He couldn't go back in time and undo it, but he could try to explain, and maybe she would understand.

"My sister is a supermodel. Do you know how many men she has dated?" Kit asked. Raw pain echoed in her voice.

"I'm guessing a lot."

"My brother is a big financier. Do you know how many women he has dated?"

Again, his answer was the same. "A number of them."

"And me, the supergeek with secrets. How many men have I dated?"

Counting the loser from the conference? She had said she'd had one significant relationship, but surely she had had other boyfriends. "A few."

"No, just the one, the man who humiliated me at Gamer Con. Do you know how that makes me feel?"

Not good. "He was an ass."

"Maybe. But he was the only man who was willing to date me."

They were walking on dicey territory. "Not everyone needs to date dozens of people."

"How many women have you dated?"

Dated? Very few. Slept with? More than he liked to admit. "Some."

"Some isn't one," she said. "When I was eight, my father told me that one day a man would fall in love with me for who I was. He told me I was beautiful, but it would take a special man to see it. He didn't have that conversation with my sister. His words made me happy at the time, but now I feel like a loser. My father recognized I was ugly and awkward. I was plenty smart. But look where that led. I've been hunted and used and tossed away."

"Stop, Kit. I don't want to hear this." He couldn't stand to hear her talk about herself this way. Her perception was skewed.

She went silent.

"I want you to listen, and I want you to listen hard. I don't care if you were an awkward teenager or didn't have a boyfriend in college or feel like a hag next to your sister. Those things are in the past and your sister is a supermodel, so don't set some impossible standard."

"She's beautiful," Kit said.

"She's a praying mantis with a pretty face. I wouldn't want to be with her because I would probably break her brittle legs."

"She has to be thin," Kit said.

"Forget about that. Let me tell you about the now, because you seem incapable of seeing it for yourself. You are a smart and capable woman who is very, very talented. You are one of the foremost computer experts in the world—so much so that the United States government hired someone to stay with you around the clock. And babe, I don't work cheap. They put a high value on you and your brain and your thoughts.

"You are a sweet woman. You give people the benefit of the doubt, like with Swish or whatever the hell his name is, and Lawrence and Zoya. Not many people who have been through what you have would keep wearing their rose-colored glasses. You know what you are protecting our country from because you had to counter it. It's an ugly, hateful world out there.

"Last, but not insignificant, is how you look. You are beautiful. I'm not talking about on the inside or in some 'every person is unique' way. I'm talking about me, walking around with a hard-on since I met you because I find you that attractive. I'm talking about nearly having to put ice in my pants the night you were drugged, because I wanted to sleep with you and take care of you how only a man could have. I think about what I want to do to you and almost all of it involves showing you how much I want you. It's not that I'm a caveman who can't control myself. It's you doing this to me. It's you, under my skin, tempting me, making me wish we were together under other circumstances, because then I would make it clear to you how much I want you."

"Griffin—"

He was hot and horny and angry. "I'm not finished." Now that he was going, he couldn't stop until she heard it all. "I'm glad other men are too stupid and too dense to find a way into your pants because that means that I've got you to myself. I don't like to share. Does it drive me crazy to know that after me, there will be some man who will make you deliriously happy? Of course it does. I'll be half tempted most of my life to look you up and find the guy you're with so I can punch him in the gut because he gets to keep you in his bed and do whatever he wants to you. I want to be that man, but I won't be. I'm married to this job, and this job is unrelenting. I can't be the man you deserve for anything longer than a night.

"So please stop knocking yourself around and thinking something is wrong with you. You are perfect how you are."

Kit said nothing. Long moments passed.

"Is it my turn to talk?" she asked.

He nodded though she could not see him. "Yes." It had felt good to get that off his chest.

She crossed the room to him. "Thank you for saying those things. Thank you for staying with me through this. Thank you for being a man who is honorable and sexy and smart and loyal. This is the most unromantic situation in the world. When I've thought about my first time with a man, I've thought about sheets and roses and food because those were the only things clear to me. But now I know that what's more important is the man and how he makes me feel.

"You make me feel desirable and sexy and beautiful. If that means that I only get a night, then fine, but it will be a great night because I know you, and you mean something to me. You started something when you found me, and you will finish it."

A prediction of future things. "That sounded like a command."

"It was," she said. "I'm not a bossy woman, but I like to have my way."

"I won't take your virginity."

She sighed. "Okay. But you will sleep beside me tonight."

He couldn't stand her hurting. Against his better judgment, he pulled her into bed next to him. She maneuvered herself to sleep in the crook of his arms.

"I have a question for you," Griffin said, sitting across from Kit while she was working on her computer. "How do you feel about secret military bases?"

Kit frowned. "Not the type of question I was hoping you'd ask. I spent too much time living on a secret base. I won't go back."

Griffin had bad news then. "The government wants us at a secret military base to secure part of the Locker and to plan the countermeasures to shut down Incognito."

A counterattack from a secure military facility with full ground, sea and air support was best.

"No," Kit said.

"You agreed to help," Griffin said.

"I agreed to help, not to spend another year of my life on a secret military base with too many rules and no freedom," Kit said.

"I am not sure we have a choice. You can't go back to your life. Incognito knows who you are, and they are looking for you."

"When I agreed to work on the Locker five years ago, it was part ego, trying to prove that I was a good computer engineer, the best hacker. But now, I've spent most of my adult life tied to a computer, and I want something else. I want something more. I've done my duty. It's someone else's turn to protect the cybersecurity of the United States."

Griffin wouldn't let it go. "It's not the same facility where you worked before."

Kit wrapped her arms around her midsection. "How would it be any different?"

"I'll be with you."

Kit met his gaze. "While that does make me feel better, it doesn't address the core issue."

"Which is?"

"I'd be walking into the same trap I walked into with the Locker. National security and what's best for the country are great. Except I gave what I could and I'm tapped out."

"While we've been looking for computer scientists to help, so has the government. They're assembling a team."

"If I am hiding on a military base for the next one or two or five years, that's a problem for me. I have plans."

He could understand her not wanting to return to that life of isolation, but what choice did she have? The West Company was working to shut down Incognito, but until they did, Kit's options were limited and she was a target. "Tell me about your plans. We can make them work regardless of what you're doing for the government."

She held out her hand and ticked items off. "My family needs to know I'm alive."

"I'll talk to Connor about that."

"I need a boyfriend."

He did not care for that idea. He'd already told her that thinking of her with another man drove him to distraction. But Connor had asked Griffin to convince her to agree to work on the Locker again. "You'll be at a military base. Men are there."

"Men like Lawrence?" she asked dryly.

"He was a traitor."

"A traitor who rejected me for Zoya," Kit said.

"You misinterpreted the situation."

She set her hands on the edges of her chair. "Which

I do a lot. You're attracted to me. I believe that you want to have sex with me."

She was correct on all counts. "We've had that conversation."

"I'll go to the military base if you sleep with me."

Griffin's jaw went slack. "That's ridiculous. We've been over this."

"You admitted you were attracted to me. You want me like I want you. Stop fighting this."

"I won't sleep with you. You deserve more."

"So you've said. Maybe I deserve a night of great sex before I'm locked away for another year of my life."

It wasn't right for him to sleep with her. She thought she wanted it, but she would see differently when she met someone who could promise her forever. Griffin didn't want to be a regret. "It might not be what you expect. You make it sound like I'm the only man…"

"You have been the only man. The only man I want to sleep with. The only man who makes me understand the word *hot*. You're doing what you love every day. You could walk into a bar and snap your fingers and ten women would take off their clothes and beg you to take them home. I can't spend another year alone, locked in a military base, working."

He grunted in frustration. "Why can't you have another online relationship?"

"Because after last night, I can't go back to something less. Make your decision and I will make mine," she said.

"I want you to go to the military base, but I won't be blackmailed."

She frowned. "Will you at least agree it's on the table?"

She was relentless, but no harm in being open to possibilities. "It's on the table. Will you come with me to work on the Locker?"

She nodded her head, but Griffin didn't feel victorious. He felt like they were agreeing to more than either of them could understand.

After a five-hour flight, the helicopter transport took two hours. Kit couldn't have guessed where they were. It was warm and humid and dark when they arrived. Somewhere tropical? The last place she had worked on the Locker had been dry and cold.

She was given a computer not yet available on the open market. She had heard whispers about it. Holding it her hands was a thrill. She felt old enthusiasm for her work creeping higher. That was likely the government's intent in giving her this computer. Fan the embers of her passion for computers and security. It had never gone away, but now she wanted her world to be more than just online.

To her chagrin, she hadn't been told more about the Locker. It was the same as when she had worked on the Locker the first time. Every scrap of information was need-to-know. No one knew everything, and most people knew almost nothing.

Upon their arrival, she and Griffin were escorted to a lab.

"He stays outside," a military guard said.

Her anxiety was too high to be left alone in a strange place. "He is my bodyguard. He comes with me."

Griffin seemed proud of her. When he stepped forward, the guard moved away.

The lab was state-of-the-art. After exploring some of the equipment, Kit worked for a few hours on the new laptop. She had blocked out the work she had done years ago on the Locker. Once she was again working on the code, details flooded back to her.

Griffin remained close, watching over her. His face was calm, but she sensed the turmoil inside him. She had caused part of it by pressing him to sleep with her. It was the right course of action, and she wouldn't be swayed.

She couldn't grow another year older and remain a virgin. When she finally found a boyfriend, a real, flesh-and-blood man, how would she explain to him her lack of experience? It wasn't a religious or cultural belief. It was a sad part of her social life that made her feel pathetic.

Would she have wanted to lose her virginity in the back of someone's truck in high school? No. Would she be willing to lose it to Griffin anytime, anyplace? An adamant yes. She needed to know she could go through with it and carry that confidence with her. She would seduce him tonight.

She turned in her chair and faced him. A hot shower and then she would find time alone with him. The benefit of being on this base was that while she had nothing to do when she wasn't working, neither did he. They just had each other.

"Why didn't you sign the confidentiality agreement?" Griffin asked.

"They need me. I don't need them. I don't need to agree to do more. I'm giving this a chance, but I'm not signing away my life." She had learned her lesson about that from the last time.

"I like this side of you. You've been bolder."

"Experience. I've been down this road. I know that I have some power. And on that note, I'm done for tonight. I need a break."

She and Griffin were escorted to their two-bedroom apartment, and Kit was pleased the dinners she had requested were on the table in their small kitchen.

Griffin sat, but he seemed distracted.

She carried the silver plate toppers to the sink. "Want to talk about it?" The sight and smell of the food should have tempted him. Grilled steak, sweet potatoes and steamed broccoli sat on their plates. He hadn't picked up his fork.

"About what?" he asked.

Why did he want to play dumb? Something was on his mind. "Are you upset that I want to sleep with you?"

"No."

Despite what he said, she heard the "yes" in his voice. An attack of conscience? Marissa had told her that men liked to eat and then have sex. Should she wait for Griffin to eat before she advanced on him?

Would he resist?

Fearing she would lose her cool or be struck by an attack of nerves if she waited, she strode to him and kissed him. His mouth opened under hers slowly, and he tipped his head back, getting a deeper angle on her mouth. She pulled away. "I'm planning to seduce you."

He lifted a brow. "You don't have to tell me. Your actions are clear."

Kit wouldn't let him make this into a joke. She knew what she wanted. With trembling hands, she removed her shirt and tossed it to the floor. Then she removed her pants and let them drop. She stepped out of them.

"Come with me," she said, and wiggled a finger at him, beckoning for him to follow her.

He stood. She pulled away the comforter and blankets and patted the bed next to her.

Griffin sat. Now what? He was allowing her to take the lead, but it would ease her anxiety if he would make this happen. They both wanted it, so why wait? She leaned forward to kiss him again and shivered when his hand went to her shoulder, stopping her.

"Don't make me say no to you. Let's eat," he said.

The sting of his rejection burned through her. She didn't want to eat, so she went for broke. "I am tired of being untouched." After what Griffin had done to her, she couldn't claim she was untouched. It seemed a silly distinction. They had crossed the line. Might as well stay over it and have some fun.

Griffin's eyes swerved from her face to her body. He swore under his breath. "Have you lost it?"

"Please touch me."

He stood from the bed and crossed the room in two long strides. "Kit, I have been thinking about touching you since the moment we met. Where your waist dips in makes me crazy. I want to fit my hands there and hold you."

"Then kiss me," she said. She was completely aroused. She wanted this. "Kiss me or I will find someone who will. I'd guess there are plenty of men here who would love the company of a woman for the night." A low blow, but she wasn't pulling punches.

He narrowed his gaze. "You wouldn't do that."

"Sure I would. You have no idea how desperate I've become. It's you I want, but if what's holding you back is my virginity, then I'll get rid of it."

He seemed livid. "Get rid of it? Kit, you are being unreasonable."

She shook her head. "I know what I want, Griffin. I want you."

He swore and then rushed to her. They came together in a tangle of arms and legs. As they tumbled onto the bed, his mouth moved seductively over hers in a slow, drugging kiss. She had made the right decision.

"I'm going to make you come until you can't breathe. You know I want you, and I am not a man who sits around and lets another have what's his." He tugged her panties down her legs and lowered himself between her thighs. He took her into his mouth. His tongue stroked and probed. The sensations were shocking, and Kit couldn't do anything except feel.

His five-o'clock shadow brushed the inside of her thighs, the gruffness in contrast with the softness of his tongue.

He alternated using his mouth and his hands. She was on the edge of another release when he stopped. She let out a whimper.

She was naked and turned on, and she wanted him. "Please."

"Say the words," he said, lowering his mouth again, pressing a kiss to her thigh and then blowing a breath of air where she wanted his mouth and his hands.

"I want to come."

He grinned and continued his caress of her body. Within minutes, he had her writhing against his mouth and at the point of rapture. Rhythmic cries shook her, and her body convulsed.

She rode the wave and felt every bone in her body relax even as her nerves tingled. "That wasn't what I had in mind."

He lay next to her, and she set her head on his chest. His erection was pressing at the leg of his pants. She rolled toward it and kissed him through the material.

He twitched, but stopped her. She shook her head. "I want more."

"Let's take our time, okay?"

"We're not leaving this room until we talk. I can sense you holding back."

"I'm trying to protect you, and I don't see the need to rush."

She ran her hand down his chest. "Don't protect

me. Not here, in this space. Just kiss me and make love to me."

Griffin wrapped his arms around her and did just as she asked. "I can do that in a hundred different ways. Let me show you."

Griffin had outlived his usefulness on this mission. They had been at the base for a week. He made Kit feel safe, but with security tight, he didn't need to be here. What was he supposed to do? Escort Kit to and from their apartment? Wait while she worked in the lab?

He needed to have a difficult conversation with Connor. Once he got clearance to fly home, he would talk to Kit about it. She would understand.

She had agreed to accompany him to the gym after work and then on a run around the area. He was curious to see what he could find and perhaps figure out where they were.

He stretched his arms, trying not to stare at her in the mirror as she climbed onto the bicycle. Lifting weights felt good. He hadn't had much time in the gym recently, and he liked staying in shape.

Once he was involved in his workout, moving and lifting distracted him from the elephant in the room. He wanted to sleep with Kit. She wanted to sleep with him. Usually, that was the green light.

Their arrangement was more complicated. She was his client. He had touched her and fooled around with her—every night since they'd arrived—and he shouldn't have. He had let their relationship progress into a gray area.

If he told Connor that he'd had sexual contact with a client, he would be fired. At least, he assumed he would. His training with the West Company hadn't covered sleeping with clients, but he knew about conflicts of interest and losing objectivity when emotions came into play.

How could they not? He had slept in Kit's bed. He had made her come with his hands and his mouth. Possessiveness was inevitable. He did not like sharing a woman with another man, just as he did not sleep with more than one woman at a time. Looking for sex elsewhere was embarrassing, like admitting one woman wasn't enough.

A few guys entered the gym. Griffin wiped down his machine and moved to one closer to Kit. Though every man and woman on this base was screened and cleared, Griffin didn't trust easily.

The West Company didn't know how far Incognito had penetrated the Locker and if they'd compromised the people who had worked with it. They had gotten to Lawrence and they could get to others, including the people who worked at this base.

The men were tossing Kit looks. Long looks. Interested looks. Kit had indicated she wanted a relationship, and Griffin had been clear he couldn't provide it. When he wasn't on the island any longer, would one of these men take his place?

The idea did not sit well with him.

Griffin strode to Kit's bike. "Ready to run?" he asked.

"Outside?" she asked, not sounding enthusiastic about the idea.

"Yes." He liked the fresh air, and working out in an air-conditioned gym wasn't the same as facing the elements.

"We can try it. But if my lungs burst, you'll have to carry me home."

He was pleased by her choice of words. To anyone listening, they sounded like a couple. Let word get around base that she wasn't available. The effect would be temporary. He had no doubt that once he left the island, she'd have her pick of men. That thought bothered him deeply. He wanted her to be happy, and he didn't like knowing that her future happiness wouldn't be with him.

Chapter 11

They left the gym, and Griffin slipped his arm across Kit's shoulders.

She looked up at the sky, a mix of gray and white clouds. "I don't run often. Maybe it will rain and save me the hassle."

"Given the humidity and the weather we've had, storms roll through quickly. A light rain might feel good."

She bent over and touched her toes, giving him a look at her shapely rear end. His body hardened, and hiding his attraction in gym shorts wasn't easy.

They followed the paved path, and he let her set the pace. The position of the sun in the sky, the heat and the stickiness of the air spoke to a tropical climate. He hadn't used his satellite phone to contact Connor yet, instead keeping his communication to approved means. He wasn't sure if the satellite phone's signal would be blacked out. "I want to get a message to Connor. I'd like to have an escape plan. If we need to get off this island, I want to know where I'm taking you for the fastest escape."

Kit touched his hand. "A little slower," she said between pants.

He'd thought she was leading. He slowed his pace and jogged beside her. In addition to his stride being twice hers, he was accustomed to running for lengthy periods of time.

"I can help you get a secure message out," Kit said.

He'd bet she could. "Have you been sending secret messages already?"

"No," she said. "I've been tempted. My family must be worried."

"They've been contacted, and they know you're safe."

"Safe? That's what this is?"

He tried not to take offense to her statement. "Do you feel secure with me?"

"I feel like I've committed a crime and am being punished. I'm not making any progress with securing the Locker or taking countermeasures against Incognito," she said. "As long as I fail at those tasks and Incognito is still strong and pervasive around the world, I'll be a target and, therefore, stuck here."

She was too hard on herself, and her rose-colored glasses were losing their tint. "It's day two. Don't get upset. If it was easy, they wouldn't need you."

"The new team doesn't know what they're doing yet," she said.

He had the sense he was more sounding board than advisor on this subject. "What makes you think that?"

"I was looking at some notes left on the message board by a teammate, and they were riddled with errors," Kit said.

The Locker was a black box. It was impenetrable. Now that was working against them.

Kit stopped running and brought her hand to her head, the other to her hip. "What if I can't fix it? What if I don't want to fix it?"

"I am sure that you can."

She shook her head. "It wasn't a one-person job."

"I understand that. But the team is just catching up. There's a learning curve."

She looked on the verge of crying. "I am good with computers. I understand them better than I understand humans. But I don't want to live here."

"No one can force you."

She said nothing to that. She started running again, and he stayed a stride behind.

They were a mile from the main facility, and Griffin heard a strange noise, like human grunting. He reached for Kit, drawing her close to him.

"What is that?" she whispered.

"I don't know." Griffin didn't see anyone, but the unmistakable sound of grunting and flesh against flesh indicated either a fight or a sexual encounter. Griffin hoped not both. "Let me look around."

If it was a fight, he could break it up. Keeping Kit in his peripheral vision, he moved through the trees.

Kit crept closer and ignored him when he waved her off.

Another few steps and someone came into view.

Not a fight. Not a sexual assault.

A couple was having sex. Loudly. A woman was perched on the bumper of a jeep, and a man was thrusting away. Both were moaning and gasping.

Kit grasped his arm. Her face was red, either from running or from embarrassment.

Without saying a word, they returned to the main path.

"That could be us," she said.

Griffin kept his composure. "I don't have any interest in being an exhibitionist."

"I didn't mean outside. I meant the sex part."

Having sex with Kit played on his mind, but he didn't voice it as an option because it wasn't. Kit didn't have a filter on her thoughts, and she was the client. She couldn't be fired for inappropriate actions.

After what they had done, how was sleeping with her any different? At least he cared about her, and he could make the night about her, concentrating on making it incredible for her. A first time that wouldn't end in disappointment or disaster. If he didn't sleep with her, she might sleep with a military man posted here or a random guy from a bar. How much satisfaction would she derive from that?

One day, she would meet a man who could appreciate how remarkable she was and who would see her intelligence and beauty and caring and want to marry her. Griffin couldn't ask her to wait to sleep with a man who would marry her, but he could make her first time one she would not forget. She wouldn't easily fall into bed with another man. He'd set her expectations high and show her what she was worth.

If he told her he wanted to leave the island and she still wanted to sleep with him, perhaps they would, now or never.

Stupidity wasn't an emotion Kit was used to feeling. She grasped complex topics with ease, and she enjoyed her work.

Now something was missing. Maybe her thoughts were too scattered and her emotions shaking her up, or maybe her heart wasn't in it this time. Headway on re-securing the Locker was slow. She hated letting someone down. Her report on her work was firmly "no progress."

The original Locker had been designed and engineered by three different people who were experts in their respective fields of computer science. How could she fill all three of those roles now? The new members of the team were smart, but without the history, they had a lot of new skills to master.

She and Griffin had arrived in their apartment after their second day of running outside after work, and Griffin had rushed to take a shower first, leaving her pacing in sweaty clothes. He was acting strangely and, typical of Griffin, he didn't discuss it. With the exception of the time he had told her that she was beautiful and that under other circumstances he'd want to be with her, he was frustratingly distant and confusing. He relayed nothing of his private thoughts.

He got out of the shower, and she slipped into the bathroom. The bathroom was serviceable but not luxurious. Kit was low-maintenance. Clean towels and basic soap were enough.

When she stepped out of the shower, she wrapped a towel around her hair and one around her body. Her clothes were in the bedroom. Quickly dressing, she hung her towels and joined Griffin in the main room.

She blinked at the transformation in the room. A brilliant array of orange, red, yellow, pink and blue flowers covered every space. Some were tucked in vases, some were scattered as individual flowers, and some petals were tossed across the floor.

Ivory candles lined the dresser.

A bottle of wine and two plates covered with silver domes were on the table.

Griffin was wearing a tuxedo, and her breath caught in her throat. She had never seen him looking this handsome.

The atmosphere left no question what this meant. A rectangular box tied with white ribbon sat on the coffee table.

He crossed the room to her, wrapped his arms around her and kissed her gently. "You smell good."

"When did you have time to do this?" she asked.

"I've had time while you were working," he said.

"I feel like I'm dressed wrong." She was wearing a blue T-shirt and navy flannel shorts because she'd thought she would eat and then go to bed.

He gestured toward the red velvet box. "Open that."

She took the gift box and untied the ribbon, lifted the lid and moved aside the tissue paper. Inside was a pair of pink pajamas made of the softest fabric. She took them from the box and held them up. The top was strappy, trimmed with lace, and the shorts were full, like a skirt.

"Give me one minute." She returned to the bathroom to change. She could have redressed in front of him, but given the amount of effort he had put into arranging this night, she didn't want to rush. Getting naked in front of him would have made them both hurry to bed.

When had Griffin changed his mind about sleeping with her? How long had he been planning this?

She changed, brushed her hair again and then returned to Griffin.

He was standing at attention, waiting for her.

"You're too dressed up." She grabbed the sides of his coat and pulled them over his shoulders. She set the black jacket over the back of the couch.

"I thought you wanted me dressed up."

"I like you in this. But I also like you with fewer clothes."

"Before this goes any further, I need to tell you something."

She waited. He had lit her on fire, and now he wanted to talk? "Tell me."

"I may be transferred to another mission."

The words hit her heavy on the shoulders. "You're leaving me."

"Nothing has been decided, but I need you to know that before this goes any further."

Their relationship had an expiration date. She could live with that. What she couldn't live with was the regret she'd harbor if he left and she had never been with him. She would wonder and wish for the rest of her life. "I understand, and it's okay. Come what may, I want this to happen tonight."

She untied his tie and unbuttoned his shirt. "Is this okay?"

"It's your night. Anything you want to do is okay with me," he said.

Anything she wanted. Where to start? She had fantasies she had never explored, role playing and old-fashioned games, but tonight she would be herself, and Griffin would be himself.

"Would you like music?" he asked.

She nodded, and he withdrew a remote from his pocket. He pressed a button, and the room was filled with soft, melodic music. He closed her in his arms again and spun her once, bringing her body flush to his. Her hips brushed his pelvis, and excitement shot through her.

It wasn't the first time they had danced together, but this time, they were alone. They didn't have the heavy pulsing of music and the grinding of bodies or the darkness of a warehouse to distract them from each other.

"I love that my body turns you on," he said.

Was it that obvious? She loved touching the hard planes of his shoulders, chest and stomach. "I could say the same."

He kissed her again, and his mouth conquered hers. His tongue demanded a response. The more he kissed her, the more she wanted him. She guided him toward the bed and pushed gently on his shoulders. When he was flat on his back, his feet on the floor, she climbed on top of him.

"Don't you want to eat first?" he asked.

She shook her head. "It will wait."

"You didn't see what I ordered for us."

"Nothing out there interests me more than what's right here."

She pressed her mouth to his and sank against him. The kiss spun into passion, and she was overcome with emotion. He tipped his hips against hers, and she responded in kind.

The soft fabric of the pajamas he'd bought her rubbed against her skin, making her feel delicate and exquisite. His hands went to her thighs and he rubbed the backs of them, massaging the muscles.

She unfastened his pants and drew them down his legs. Button by button, she removed his shirt. He sat and took the hem of her camisole by the narrow strip of lace and pulled it over her head. He dropped it and then closed his mouth over her exposed nipple.

His hand caressed her and his mouth moved between her breasts until she was hot and achy. Shockingly sensuous feelings tumbled over her. Her head hit the pillow and she melted into the mattress. He removed the rest of her clothes.

The haze of sharp lust took over. She wanted this to last forever, yet she wanted him to hurry and give her the fulfillment she craved. Skin to skin, sensations pulsed between them.

He moved on top of her, donned a condom and then let his weight settle over her. He rocked his hips, the head of his arousal pressing at the V of her legs, but not entering her.

He reached between them and used his hands to heighten her excitement. She was ready, and she lifted her hips, encouraging him to push inside her. He pulled back. "Easy. We have all night."

All night? Scorching desire pricked at her, and the more he touched her, the more she wanted him. She grabbed his hips and parted her thighs. "Take me or I will take you."

His eyes burned with heat and he pushed inside her, just a little. He stretched her and he worked his hips, moving inside her, deeper and deeper. "This might hurt."

She was ready. Hot and wet, she set her hands on his hips and drew him closer.

He surged forward, and a sharp pain shot between her legs. He stilled and she shifted, searching for a more comfortable position. Tears sprang to her eyes, and she blinked them back. One escaped and Griffin kissed it, then wiped it away with his thumb.

"Are you okay?" he asked, his voice tender and warm.

She nodded.

He kissed her, deep kisses, hard kisses, soft kisses, and caressed her. The pain between her legs subsided, and other needs grew more pressing. "Please, Griffin, make love with me."

She stayed with him in the moment, watching him move, trying to remember every detail of this night so she could recall it later.

He moved languidly inside her, his strokes deep and slow. Lust wound tight inside her.

He touched her cheek, the most delicate of touches, running his hand down to her chin. "You are so beautiful."

Holding her close, he set a hard and steady rhythm, plunging deep, making her crazier by the second. Pressure built inside her.

She dug her fingers into his shoulders, holding on, anchoring herself. She was lost to Griffin. Her body, her heart, her everything. She had been on the edge of loving him and now, with the unspeakable perfection of this act, she knew. No going back, not for her heart. She had fallen in love with him.

She held his hips, stilling him inside her. More than she wanted to finish, she wanted to talk.

"What's the matter? Are you hurt?" he asked. A

sheen of sweat glistened on his forehead, and she knew he must be exerting control to remain unmoving.

"Not hurt. I want to look at you for a minute. I want you to tell me that this means something to you." She needed to know. It was important to her, and he had said this night was about her.

"I thought long and hard before I took this step with you. I don't want to hurt you. I want you to remember your first time and feel happiness."

She smiled. His thoughtfulness had to be enough for now. She released his hips. He pumped into her and she wrapped her legs around him, accepting him as part of her. Griffin, the delicious scent of him, his handsome face, her love for him, were too much. They overwhelmed her, and she shattered in his arms. He rode her as her orgasms played out.

He held her tight in his arms, the weight of him pressing her into the mattress. She kissed his chest. "That was the best I've ever had."

He laughed at her joke. "Can I leave you here for a minute and get you something to clean up?"

She nodded and stretched in the bed, feeling pleased with herself. When he returned with a warm washcloth, he cleaned the inside of her thighs.

He brought the food to the bed and they ate, talked and laughed. He was a friend to her, her protector and her lover. Being in love with him was a natural progression of their relationship. But he wouldn't be part of her life long. He would be assigned to another mission, another adventure, and leave her behind.

She couldn't talk herself out of loving him even with that realization, even though hurt waited for them at the end of their time together.

Kit could cause massive trouble by calling her sister, but she needed to talk to Marissa. Griffin would be pissed. Connor would be furious. The security of the Locker was at stake.

But even though her sister didn't understand her, her sister understood men.

Kit didn't have her personal cell phone—that had been taken long before—but she spoofed the call to appear from her regular number. Otherwise, her sister wouldn't answer. Marissa received far too many solicitation calls.

"Hello?" Her sister sounded afraid.

"Don't say my name, but it's Kit."

"So—" She let out her breath in a rush. "Do you know people are looking for you? Are you safe? Where are you? What's going on?"

Guilt shot through her. "You were supposed to be told I was safe."

She could hear her sister's heels clicking against the floor as she paced. "Some guy with a government ID came over and told us you were safe. But he explained nothing. We asked questions and he only said it was a matter of national security. I've been worried. Who were those men at the party? What's going on? Did you witness a crime? Was your boss at the florist involved in a financial scam?"

Kit didn't have much time before someone realized

she'd hacked into their communication system to call her sister. "I can't explain everything, but I am safe." For now. "I need your advice. I'm in love."

Marissa gasped. "You ran away to be with a man?"

"I didn't run away. I've been in protective custody, and the man assigned to protect me is really special."

"Are you in love with your kidnapper? Do you have Stockholm syndrome?" Marissa asked.

Her sister was being melodramatic. "Again, I wasn't kidnapped."

"Mom will be relieved you're okay."

"You can't tell Mom I called."

Marissa shrieked. "Are you kidding? She's having a fit about you being gone."

Kit didn't think her mother would have thought much of it. Her mother usually acted like she was an embarrassment to the family. "I'll send a message through my protector to her, but I need your help. Marissa, I don't have a lot of time."

"Tell me what I can do. Anything."

"How do I make a man fall in love with me?" The question was ridiculous, and Kit hated asking that way. Time restraints meant she had to be direct.

"Does he reciprocate your feelings at all?" Marissa asked.

Last night had made her wonder. Griffin had said they couldn't sleep together, but then they had. Had he changed his mind because he had fallen for her, too? "I don't know. I think somewhat. We have chemistry."

"Chemistry is good, but it can change. If you want

him to love you, you need to have fun with the chemistry, but also let him get to know you."

How would that help? "He knows me pretty well. He dressed up in a costume for me."

"Kinky. Like a sex costume?"

In a sense, yes, but she couldn't admit that to her sister. "As a character from a video game."

"He didn't run away screaming when you told him about your love of video games?" Marissa asked.

"He was into it." At least, he hadn't complained.

"Then maybe he's in love, too."

"He had to dress up."

"I'm trying to imagine a scenario where a man is forced to dress up and I'm coming up empty, unless this was on a set. He isn't required to do anything. If he dressed up, he wanted to for you."

"Men don't usually fall for me." The incident with Swift came rushing back, and anger was the stronger emotion over embarrassment.

"You're selling yourself short. Lots of men are interested in you. You don't want to see it. You avoid eye contact, and you make excuses to leave conversations. I've been trying to tell you for years that you give these signals like you aren't interested, so men don't pursue you."

She started to deny it, but shut her mouth because it was true. She hated social gatherings, and anyone who met her knew it. "He's leaving soon. Our circumstances aren't permanent."

"I've had a lot of men love and leave me. Here's what I've learned. If he leaves, then it wasn't meant to be, and you will find someone else. But the man who's meant to stick around and be with you won't leave. He'll find a way to stay regardless of what happens or what commitments he has. Of course, as I say this, I realize that no man has ever decided to stick around for me. I have hope it will happen with the right man at the right time."

"You have men falling all over you," Kit said.

"I have men interested in my fame and fortune. Few stick around and actually want to be with me."

It was the first time her sister had shared an insecurity. "Should I tell him that I love him?"

"Being that direct might freak him out. Let your actions show it. Once you say those words, you can't take them back, and if he doesn't feel the same, it could chase him away. I'm really happy for you, Kit. I've been hoping that someone would get inside your walls. I can't wait to meet this man. He must be something special."

Griffin most certainly was. But could Kit keep him in her life?

Kit was alone in the lab. Alone except for Griffin, who was working on something on his computer. The hum of the computer fans and the air-conditioning created a soothing white noise. But Kit still felt agitated. She and the team were not making progress as she had planned, and she sensed information was being held back. The less she knew, the longer they would be at this, trapped on this island, trying to find the security holes in the Locker and close them and to find the locations of Incognito's version of the Locker.

It was past five o'clock, and the other engineers on the team had returned to their apartments for the day. Kit had stayed because she needed the quiet to think. The team lobbed questions at her all day, and the constant interruptions made progress slow. She could share what she knew and being that open was refreshing, but explaining the details of the Locker wasn't simple. The skill sets of the engineers varied, and Kit wasn't masterful at communicating.

The project manager continually pressed her for dates when she would have accomplished significant progress. He also asked if he could get her anything to help.

She tried to be diplomatic and evasive, but she wanted to scream that it would take as long as it took and he could help her by not interrupting her ten times a day with inane questions.

Being near Griffin was distracting. Not that he said much to her in the lab unless she spoke to him. Having him around made her want to shorten her hours and spend more time with him. She didn't voice those thoughts because if he were pulled from the project, she would be destroyed. She didn't want to be on this island, but having Griffin with her made it bearable.

"What are you working on?" she asked, turning in her chair.

Griffin looked up from his computer screen, his

green eyes serious. "I have the mission specs for my next assignment."

His next assignment? Was he bailing on her soon? Her stomach dropped. "When does it start?"

"As soon as possible."

"Are you leaving?" she asked.

"When you don't need me anymore," he said.

She needed him, and she couldn't put an end date on that. He was her strength and her friend, and it had taken her whole lifetime to connect with someone the way she'd connected with him. How did he feel about her? Her body was sore from the nights in bed with him and those memories were so fresh, she had trouble believing that he felt nothing for her.

How could he hold her and make love with her and then tell her he was thinking about his next mission, a mission that didn't include her? What would happen when they parted ways? Would she be able to speak to him? Was Griffin Brooks his real name? If he didn't want to be contacted, he could make that happen.

"What's the mission?" she asked. She heard shrillness in her voice and tried to calm herself. She had to play it cool.

"I can't discuss that," he said.

She'd expected an evasive answer but had hoped it would open the dialogue between them. "Does it involve getting punched?" When they had first met, he had been punched a number of times.

He laughed. "I would say there's a high probability of that happening."

Her thoughts jumped to other unpleasant scenarios. Would it involve him meeting someone else? Having an affair with another woman? Kit felt sick to her stomach. She turned back to the computer, but she was too distracted by what Griffin had said to continue working. She stared at the screen for a few more minutes and then tried again. "Griffin." She didn't know what else to say to him. So many words overwhelmed her.

He looked at her with intensity blazing in his eyes. "You can tell me anything. Say what you need to say."

She wished she had the words to express what she was feeling. Her anxiety and nervousness about the project persisted. Having Griffin nearby made her feel safe and sane.

He came closer. "Are you hurt?"

The room was under surveillance, and she didn't want to have this conversation here. "Can we go home? I'm not making progress, and it's frustrating."

He nodded. "You might feel better after dinner."

Unlikely food would change anything, but in their place, they could talk without security watching them. She could be more open and honest, assuming she had the courage to speak her mind.

Kit gathered her belongings, and they followed the security procedures to checkout. Every item they took from the lab had to be screened.

Griffin walked her home, though he didn't hold her hand or touch her. After the nights they'd spent together, that stung. If they had a relationship, why was he hiding it? Was he worried what his boss would think? Was he embarrassed to be seen with her?

Kit felt the urge to throw herself into his arms. Instead, she threw down. "You *want* to leave. You *want* to go on another mission." One that was likely far away from her. A fresh start for him, a stinging loss for her.

"You don't need me here."

She arched a brow at him. "How so? Incognito is still looking for me."

"You're safe here. There's military crawling all over this place."

Except she didn't feel safe with soldiers. Lawrence had been a soldier and had turned on them, selling her and Zoya out to Incognito. "We haven't destroyed the copy of the Locker, and I haven't secured the new one or launched a counterattack."

"You will." He sounded certain.

She narrowed her eyes at him. "While I appreciate the vote of confidence, I think you're looking for a reason to leave."

"Why would I want to leave?"

She threw her hands in the air. "This was never what you set out to do. You were supposed to bring me in and leave me at a safe house for someone else to handle. That didn't happen because Incognito is good. Too good. They've outsmarted us too many times. I made you stay with me, but I saw in your face that you didn't want to. I needed you to stay."

"You don't need me," he repeated.

Kit felt as if she were staring at him from across a huge divide. "That's where you're wrong." She needed him like she needed the air around her. He was a constant in her life, the person she could look to when life was rough. "I need you."

He looked at her unblinking, completely emotionless. "There's a reason I work in extraction and retrievals. I'm not a bodyguard. I've been playing one, but our luck will run out."

She couldn't talk to him when he was like this. Shaking off the hurt, she turned away. "I have work."

She needed space from him, somewhere to be alone.

"I thought you wanted dinner at home," he said.

"Suddenly, I'm not hungry." He was in a mood to ice her out, and she wasn't in the mood to oblige.

"Are you returning to the lab?" he asked.

"Yes."

"I have to come with you."

"I thought you said I didn't need you. If I'm safe here, then you might as well take a break."

"Kit, don't be like this. What happened between us was great, but how long can this last? I sit in a lab and watch you work. We're surrounded by trained military men and women. Have you considered how boring that is for me?"

"Then that's the reason. You're bored here."

He shook his head. "You've known from the beginning that my area of expertise is not in protection. I want to be placed where I can do some good."

He was doing good. He had saved her on multiple occasions. "I don't want you to leave and take a new assignment."

"That isn't up to you. Not entirely," Griffin said.

"Who makes the call?" Kit asked.

"Connor West."

Kit could call Connor and express her desire to have Griffin stay with her, but trapping Griffin wasn't in her best interest. He would resent her unless he made the decision himself. Why couldn't she convince him to stay? What were the words he needed to hear?

"I'll be safe in the lab. Please, give me some space," she said.

She returned to the lab and didn't look back. She ignored the guard who checked her in, seeing that he was the man who had out-processed her a few minutes before.

She entered her lab and sat down at the computer.

Kit had worked long, late nights on the Locker years before. She couldn't count the number of nights she was alone in the lab, working all night, but it had to be hundreds. It was how she worked best. Now it depressed her. This wasn't the life she wanted. She didn't find constant solitude appealing.

Even working in the greenhouse had been more fulfilling. She craved privacy at times but acknowledged a difference between being alone and loneliness.

As she worked, her thoughts wandered to Griffin. Why was she pushing him for answers? Her sister had advised her to show Griffin she cared for him. She had done the opposite. He had baggage, and until he was ready to put it down, it would burden him.

She dove into her work, concentrating on the parts

of the Locker she had control over. Something about this part of the Locker she was working on seemed different. As she scrolled through the code, she realized that the Locker must be housed somewhere local. The calls were over a local area network. She considered interesting possibilities.

A red light high on the wall flashed, interrupting her. She turned to the monitoring screen hung near the door. The words Unauthorized Overhead Activity scrolled across the screen with no further information given. A plane off its flight path? She had been through several false alarms in the past. When working out of a secure location, any unknown was cause for investigation. It was usually nothing.

A sense of dread washed over her when the light didn't stop after a few moments. She didn't know the policies and procedures of this base, but red flashing warnings were bad. She strode to the door and pressed her fingers over the biometric lock to open it. If the base went into lockdown mode, she didn't want to be trapped in this room alone for hours or days. She wanted to be near Griffin. The door slid open.

Griffin was sitting on the floor, and surprise shook her. He rose to his feet, and her annoyance with him dissipated.

"Overhead activity," she said.

"I saw the alert. Couldn't get into the lab without you and the guard told me the most he'd allow was to let me wait out here. Until we know what's happening, we should move somewhere safe. The guard left his post, likely to find out what is happening."

"It could be friendly traffic," she said. Her experiences in the past told her it was probable.

"I don't want to wait around to find out," Griffin said. This time he took her hand in his. She found comfort in his touch.

A shrill alarm sounded. The situation was escalating.

Chapter 12

Griffin pulled Kit toward the exit. "Come on."

"Where are we going?" she asked. She didn't have a plan. Their apartment wasn't necessarily the best place to wait. They had little information to go on.

His face was intense, like it was every time they were in danger. "I have a plan."

How could he think he wasn't a good protector? He took the job seriously, and he was engaged in finding a safe place for her. Kit's head spun. "We have to stay here. We can lock the door to the lab." Panic was setting in. How close was the danger? Being in the lab with Griffin wasn't as scary as being there alone.

"I'm not locking us in a room and waiting for someone to bomb their way in and then slaughter us."

That sobering thought cut through her panic.

"Lead the way." She had trusted Griffin before, on many levels, and she would trust him now.

They fled the lab. Outside the building, the sky was dark and quiet. Had it been a false alarm? A test?

"I'm scared," Kit said.

"I won't let anything happen to you." He touched the side of her face and pressed a kiss to her lips.

Her love for him and the trust she had in him swelled inside her. "I know you won't."

Griffin hadn't liked this place from the day they'd arrived. The secret location and the lack of information had made his skin crawl. What was occurring? Did he want to know?

"We need supplies. We need the satellite phone. Connor will give us a straight answer," Griffin said.

They ran toward their apartment. Griffin kept a backpack stocked with necessary items. If they were to survive in the wilderness for a time, he needed the bare minimum: a knife, striker and flint and a compass or his watch.

They hurried into the apartment, and Griffin grabbed his pack and his satellite phone.

Someone knocked on their door, and Griffin pointed to his bedroom. He didn't want to be taken somewhere to wait. He wanted to be free to move around at his discretion. They ran into the bedroom and climbed out through the window.

They ran. Griffin and Kit found a place to hide in the jungle in sight of the base. His first call was to Connor.

"We heard a message that the base was investigating overhead activity, and now there seems to be panic all around us," Griffin said.

He heard Kate's voice in the background. "Let me find out what's going on. Are you and Kit safe?" Connor asked.

"For now," Griffin said. "We're on our own, though." As a West Company operative, he worked alone on many assignments. While he liked to assist others, he had learned not to rely on them. He could make faster, better decisions alone.

"Kate says she sees a boat moving toward the island. Not a United States vessel. And we see air traffic."

"Where are we? I haven't tracked our location on the sat phone," Griffin said.

"Military base on an unmapped island off the coast of southern California," Connor said. "The base sees the approaching vessel, too. They have alerts going out for sea and air support."

"What's my next move?" Griffin asked.

"Get Kit and yourself off that island," Connor said. "If you can't do that before you're trapped, you'll need a place to lie low and hide out. I'll send an extraction team."

"Ten-four," Griffin said.

"We'll message you as information becomes available," Connor said.

Griffin disconnected the call. He had thoughts similar to Connor's—either to run or wait for the crisis to pass. Griffin wasn't a fool. He didn't wait around for a problem to explode in his face. He knew where a few helicopters were stored, gassed and ready to fly. It would take time to get to the location, but the sooner he did, the better. He could avoid the air attacks and fly Kit to safety.

"Maybe it's nothing. I don't see anything," Kit said. Her fingernails were digging into his arm. Some of the noise seemed to have subsided. The military on this island might react to every unknown or threat like DEFCON 1 due to the sensitive intel they were guarding.

A whistling sound cut through the air. Griffin reached for Kit, tucking her against him. That sound was too familiar. Ammunition was being fired, far enough from them to avoid the energy wave, close enough to see the fireball rise in the darkening sky.

This was not a drill. Drills didn't involve live missiles.

The base was organizing. All the soldiers knew their roles and where they needed to be. Could they counter this attack? The nearest help could be an hour or more away.

A plane roared overhead and rained bombs down. Their target was likely buildings. The jungle was safer.

"The Locker. They'll steal the rest of it," Kit said.

"Doesn't matter. What matters is your safety," Griffin said.

Kit jerked away from him. "It does matter. If Incognito acquires a copy of the entire system, they'll have access to every classified document the United

States wants kept under wraps. We're putting people at risk—CIA agents undercover, NSA operations overseas and black ops around the world."

They needed to focus on the life-and-death situation in front of them—namely, Kit's life. "We'll worry about it later after we get ourselves out of here," Griffin said.

Kit's face was a mix of fear and resolve. "We'll worry about it now. I need access to the underground shelter on the west side of the island."

He didn't know what she was talking about. "What's there?"

"An access point to the Locker. I've been remoting into it from the lab. I figured out today that the island houses a piece of the Locker that's running live. I can access it directly and maybe protect it."

They'd have to run through the jungle to an inexact location to accomplish what she was proposing. "How fast can you work?"

He heard the rat-tat-tat of gunfire from the overhead planes and the retaliation from the ground. Shouting and blasts surrounded them. They could be caught in the middle of the attack. He hadn't decided if he should throw her over his shoulder and force her off the island or let her work on the Locker from the access point. The Locker was likely housed in a secure area. Secure enough to provide shelter during this bombing?

In the dimness of the night, Griffin glimpsed several boats gliding through the water toward the island. More assailants would be on the shore in thirty minutes. The boats could launch their own attacks against the island. Where had Incognito gained access to boats and planes for a military-style attack? With enough money, anything could be bought, but Griffin hadn't realized Incognito was that prosperous and well-connected.

"How did we not have warning about this?" Griffin asked.

"The Locker. Incognito has already hacked in, controlling what we can see. They are manipulating at least part of it. If they gain control of the final piece, we're screwed. They can manipulate our systems, and our military is heavily reliant on certain technologies to stay ahead of the enemy. If the enemy is inside, it's harder to defend."

Terrifying implications. "If I get you to the access point, can you fix this? Can you give control of the Locker back to the Americans?" he asked.

Kit pressed her hands together and brought them to her forehead. "I don't know. I want to say yes. I know you want me to say yes. But I don't know."

He made a quick decision based on instinct more than logic. "Only one way to find out. I'll get you there, and you'll do your best."

Her best might not be enough. The Locker had been created and engineered by the sharpest minds in the world. It was built to prevent intrusions and stop attempts at disabling it. It had been compromised. What could she do now?

She had to shut down the Locker and keep it from

being copied or used against them. But what about the files—and the people—it was protecting?

Incognito could already be copying every kilobyte of data they could access. American agencies and the Department of Defense had been relying on the Locker to handle their security threats and concerns. Without it, many people were in danger. Undercover identities and top secret missions would be made public knowledge.

It was humid, and the sounds of whistling and explosions filled the air. An airplane burst into flames overhead, debris showering down.

Griffin held her against him. "Are you sure it's worth taking the time to look for the Locker?"

Kit couldn't let the Locker be turned against them. "It's worth it."

"Tell me what to look for," Griffin said.

"I remember some specifications from the original design. The location won't be too close to the shoreline, because it's underground and that would make keeping it dry harder. It would pull a significant amount of power, and while it might run over a wireless connection, there will be at least some cables running to the bunker for light and air conditioning," Kit said.

"If it needs power, we'll start at the generator. We'll follow the lines to the bunker," Griffin said.

A great plan. "Agreed."

The power station would be a target for Incognito to strike at, as was their modus operandi. Taking it out would result in more panic.

Kit stepped up her pace, determination driving her.

The power station was small but efficient. While generators were installed around the island, running on propane, solar and gasoline, the prime energy source was this location. The Locker would have secondary backup power sources.

Guards were on post, watching the sky. She and Griffin didn't need to get inside the power station. They made a wide perimeter around the station and found several heavy power lines leading away from it.

"Which one should we follow?" Kit asked. They were pressed for time, and making the wrong decision would cost them.

"Based on where they're leading, I'm thinking that one," Griffin said.

The line Griffin had selected was running away from the beach. "It was my top pick, too."

Griffin adjusted his backpack on his shoulders. "Let's go, then."

The farther they moved through the jungle, the more Kit welcomed the coolness of the night air. If only the air wasn't so still. The power line had disappeared underground and they had continued in the same direction, hoping it led to the Locker.

Griffin handed her a water bottle. "Drink."

She accepted it and took a long swallow. "Are you sure we aren't walking in circles?"

"Not according to my compass," Griffin said.

"Can we take a break for a few minutes?" Kit asked. They had been keeping a relentless pace, and while Griffin seemed comfortable, Kit wasn't in nearly as good shape.

Without waiting for an answer, she sat on the ground. "Watch for fire ants," Griffin said.

She rose quickly and brushed at her arms. "Now my skin is crawling."

"Were you bitten?" Griffin asked.

"No. But I hate being outdoors."

"Hadn't noticed," Griffin said. "Focus on finding the bunker and what you'll do when we arrive. We don't know how much time we'll have. We won't be the only ones looking for it."

Kit brushed her hair away from her face. She had been composing a list of steps and tricks to try if any of them didn't work. "Is this exciting enough work for you?"

Griffin stared at her for a long moment. "My primary concern is your safety."

"How would I do this without you?" She needed him. She always would. Why couldn't he see that?

"We should get moving. When it gets pitch-black, it will be that much harder to search."

He didn't want to discuss it. Point taken. Kit followed behind him, trying not to fixate on his blow-off. Why was it so hard for him to talk about problems?

The bunker announced itself with a two feet high metal gate about twenty feet in diameter. The hum of the ground near the circle indicated something was happening in this area, likely a power source, an air-conditioning unit and water control. "This has to be it," Kit said.

"Or it's a sewage collection area and we're about to get a very disgusting surprise," Griffin said.

Kit dug for the access panel. She had to get the bunker open. "Help me look. There should be an access panel somewhere. The lock is electronic. My prints should open it."

Griffin helped her dig in the dirt around the perimeter, moving leaves and twigs. They found the lock two feet from the bunker, covered in layers of rotting leaves and mud. Kit twisted off the top of the panel to access the biometric reader.

She prayed it would accept her fingerprints.

"Get your hands in the air." A voice with a thick accent.

Kit glanced over her shoulder. Not American soldiers. Three of Incognito's mercenaries had made it to the island, and they had found the bunker, too. She and Griffin were in trouble, outnumbered and outgunned.

Kit was useless in a fight, but she had to destroy the Locker. Better to disable it than let it fall into enemy hands.

"We're here for the Locker and Kit Walker. Don't make this harder than it needs to be." The man who had issued the first threat had spoken. He was the tallest and largest in the group.

"Kit is spoken for." Griffin sprang into action.

Kit had seen Griffin fight, but she was riveted by how he moved. He disarmed the leader first, taking his gun from him and landing several punches and kicks. The man fell to the ground. Without the instructions of their leader, one of the men rushed at Griffin and the other at her. Griffin grabbed her attacker before he could touch her, earning himself a punch to the face by the other.

"Get in that bunker and do what you need to do!" Griffin said, still wrestling with the last assailant.

Kit laid her hand over the access panel and punched in her PIN.

Griffin stumbled back, blood pouring from his cheek. Her heart twisted violently, and anger rose inside her.

Griffin took a kick to the stomach and grabbed the man's leg, lifting him, twisting and slamming his body to the ground.

Kit heard the lock disengage on the bunker.

Throwing branches and brushing leaves from the door, she tugged on the handle. The door was stuck, rusty and heavy. She pulled with everything she had.

Griffin grabbed hold and hauled it open.

"You're bleeding," she said. Blood ran from his cheek. It was too dark to assess his injuries fully, but he had taken every hit meant for her.

"I'm fine. Get to work. I'll guard you."

"You're staying out here?" she asked.

"Incognito knows about the bunker, and they know who you are and that you're here. You're in grave danger. Destroy the Locker. Quickly."

With trembling legs, Kit descended the narrow ladder into the bunker. She fell the last three feet, slipping on the metal. The small room, four by four, smelled of wet earth, but the equipment was sealed in plastic containers and vented through a pipe be-hind them.

"Any progress?" Griffin's voice.

She hadn't touched the computer. Focusing, she stood in front of the retinal scanner and placed her hand on the fingerprint reader. A keyboard slid out from the system. How had Incognito bypassed the biometric security on the other pieces of the Locker?

The weight of her actions pressed down on her. If she disabled the Locker, lives were at stake. If she didn't, Incognito would take complete control of it and master it, and the result was the same. Worse, they would use the full power of it against the United States.

Her heart pounded. She had to find another so-lution.

Every attempt to access top secret systems passed through the Locker, checking credentials. There was no other way to obtain classified documents.

If she barraged the Locker with requests for ac-cess, the Locker would register too many requests as a brute force attack and lock everything down. It would issue a warning to the system owners of the suspected attack and to take the systems it protected off-line.

Could she simulate a brute force attack and trip the Locker into lockdown mode? It would be a major problem for system administrators at the CIA, NSA, FBI and black ops. It was the best solution under the circumstances.

She searched for unsecured computers on the net-work, which would be suspicious to the Locker. She wrote a shell script to send requests for document access. Millions of requests, one after another from a dozen computers.

"We have more visitors," Griffin said. He closed the door to the bunker. The only light was from the computer screen. In the lower right-hand corner was a star, a nod to the mastermind behind the Locker. Stargazer had gone absolutely stark-raving mad during the project and had been hospitalized. He'd tried to kill himself twice. The pressure this project had put on the team had been immense. Was she destined for the same fate as Stargazer and Arsenic? Either a life on the run or a life in a sanatorium?

She could hear gunfire and shouting. Was Griffin safe?

With her scripts running and generating increasing traffic loads, she scaled the rungs of the ladder and opened the hatch.

Griffin was now bleeding from his mouth. His body would be covered in bruises. Unconscious or dead bodies littered the ground around him.

"I'm finished. I am forcing the Locker to shut down access to every classified system in the United States."

"Won't that cause a problem?"

Many angry bureaucrats and senators and system administrators. Military groups would move to their downtime procedures and be stuck using less than real-time data. "It was our best option."

"Then let's beat feet. We're not safe yet."

* * *

The helicopter Griffin had pinpointed as an escape method was miles away. Those miles would be dangerous, taking them back toward the main base, where the fighting had been most fervid. Griffin had nothing to disguise her. Finding a military uniform would be impossible in the chaos. Hiding could leave them cornered, and if the bombing continued, the area would lay in ruins.

Griffin had most of his rounds in his gun. He would save them for when they were necessary to protect Kit.

Jogging along the path, Kit stopped, panting, resting her hands on her knees. "I need to break. Just for a minute. I need to think."

"If you don't run, I'll carry you. Come on, Kit, you can do this." She had done so well. She wasn't accustomed to working in war zones, and her body wasn't primed for long bouts of exertion. He needed to keep her motivated. Surviving this was a mental game, and mental quickness and sharpness were things Kit had in spades. He tried to tap into that. "I've seen you do the impossible. Let's take this all the way."

She accepted his outstretched hand and ran behind him. The sound of off-road vehicles approaching cut through the gunfire. Griffin pulled Kit off the main path. Branches scratched at him as he moved into the vegetation. He tried to protect her from the brush. He squatted on the ground, watching and using the leaves and green to blend.

Unmarked vehicle after vehicle passed them. Had

they been deployed to protect physical access to the Locker? Were they part of the United States military or Incognito's mercenaries?

"Any chance they can undo whatever you did?" Griffin asked.

She shook her head. "I need the sat phone."

He handed it to her and she started typing.

"What are you doing?" he asked.

"Checking if my plan worked," she said. "Which it did." Relief emanated from her voice.

"Do you have a way to show a satellite image above us? It'll be rough getting to the chopper blind."

She twisted her lips in thought. "Overhead images were distorted by the Locker as an additional security measure. I could redirect an active satellite to fly over. With the Locker down, we can get an accurate picture." She had a mischievous look in her eyes.

"We've pissed off most of the intelligence community today. Why not piss them off a little more?" Griffin asked.

He wouldn't make excuses for the choices he and Kit had made to protect themselves and the Locker. They had done the best they could with the resources they had. He doubted that would stand up in court if charges were filed, but he couldn't think about that now. *Treason.* It was an ugly word, but heads would roll over this and likely, his would be one of them.

When the vehicles were out of sight, he and Kit ventured back onto the path. Kit held the phone, looking at the display. She pointed ahead. "Let's continue in this direction and wait for the phone to receive the redirected input."

Vehicle noises sounded on the road. They took shelter and waited for them to pass.

A twig snapped behind him. Griffin turned. A man in dark camo was approaching, a knife in one hand and a gun in the other. Griffin moved in front of Kit.

The assailant's dark green outfit gave nothing away. Was he with Incognito or an American?

"Not another step," Griffin said.

The man said something he didn't understand but pointed at Kit and spoke her name. When he lifted his arm, his sleeve moved, revealing a spear tattoo. Incognito. Using his gun would bring other Incognito mercenaries running in their direction.

Griffin kicked the man's gun from his hand. It flew overhead and disappeared into the foliage. The assailant swung his knife, and Griffin dodged it. The man stabbed forward and Griffin pivoted, grabbing his arm, breaking it and slamming the assailant's forearm against his knee, forcing the knife out of his hand.

The assailant screamed in pain. Griffin robbed him of his comm device. "Kit, let's move." No reason to kill the Incognito operative. Without his device, he couldn't call for backup. A bonus was having access to the enemy's communication system.

He and Kit kept a brisk pace. The chopper was in this vicinity, but it was increasingly harder to gain his bearings in the darkness.

Kit caught his arms. "Griffin, I messed with some big, important systems. I locked out applications that people rely on. Someone will be punished for this. Someone will have to take the blame, and that someone will be me."

He wouldn't let her shoulder the blame. "I'll cop to it. Or you and I can disappear for a few months and let the anger die down. Then I'll step forward and take responsibility."

Kit pressed a finger over his lips. "A few months or a year won't make a difference. My credentials were used. The government will know it was me. I'm looking at jail time, and I need to say this to you. Thank you for what you've done for me. Thank you for keeping me safe. I never expected it, but I've fallen in love with you. I love you, Griffin."

She'd pulled the pin on an emotional grenade and lobbed it in his direction. This was an extraordinary situation, and she was scared and tired. "You're not in love with me." If it wasn't the situation bringing emotions to the surface, it was the sex. They'd had great sex. Once-in-a-lifetime sex. Sex wasn't love, and she was confusing the two.

Her jaw slackened, and she set her hand over her heart. "How can you say that to me? You don't know how I feel."

He sensed a fight brewing and wanted to diffuse it. This wasn't the time or place to argue. "You're right. I don't know how you feel. I think you're misinterpreting what we have for love."

She shook her head. "You are making this hard when it's a simple thing."

Relationships were never simple. So many responsibilities and obligations he couldn't fulfill. Beth had died. Griffin hadn't been able to protect her. "We'll talk about this later."

Her hand sliced through the air. "There might not be a later, Griffin. That's why I wanted to say it to you now."

Griffin shook off the heaviness that sat on his shoulders. "We'll survive this. I won't consider other options."

A cramp in her side and a fracture in her heart. Griffin didn't love her. He never would. He didn't believe that she loved him.

Why had she said anything? Kit should have kept her trap shut and hoped that they would eventually find themselves together and out of danger. That would have been a better time to evaluate her emotions and talk with Griffin. But she'd rushed into the confession, not thinking he would outright deny her feelings or reject her.

The weight of what she had done to the Locker settled onto her. The heads of the CIA, FBI, NSA and black ops would be furious with her. They might send assassins for her. They'd want someone punished.

She doubted they'd wait for an explanation why she had made a drastic decision without consulting anyone. She hadn't had time to give a warning. She wouldn't have known whom to alert.

As for Griffin, she had spoken words that couldn't be taken back. Her sister had warned her to let her actions lead the way. Kit had instead tossed her heart to him.

They saw the hangar before they could see the planes and helicopters waiting on the tarmac. The airfield was busy. Hundreds of people running in various directions.

"How will we get to the chopper?" Kit asked.

"Confidence. There's chaos around us. Walk onto the airstrip quickly, purposefully, and get into the helicopter. Don't look around, and don't make eye contact with anyone."

"It can't be that easy."

"It's the best-case scenario. For us. Let's hope it works. Otherwise, follow my lead and I'll get us out of this."

"Do you have a plan B?" Kit asked.

"Not at the moment, but we'll think of something."

She loved his confidence. She was a planner. She liked having a schedule and knowing her tasks. This situation was ambiguous and ever-changing. Taking a page from her sister, Kit strutted onto the airstrip.

Incognito must not know of the airstrip's existence, or it must have been heavily defended, since it was not under fire. Griffin pointed to the small chopper sitting unattended.

It looked old and the paint was faded, but Griffin seemed undeterred.

Griffin took her hand and helped her into the helicopter. He climbed in after her and sat in the pilot's seat.

"Do you know what you're doing?" Kit asked.

"I'm stealing a helicopter from the United States military."

Her heart raced at his words. Griffin started the engine. The whirl of the blades drew attention, and military men rushed toward them, shouting at them to stop.

No turning back now. Kit prayed they would make it off the island.

The helicopter lifted off the ground. Griffin put on headphones and pointed to a set in front of her. She slipped them over her ears. As Griffin moved away from the hangar, Kit considered the possibility they would be shot down. Griffin seemed to be flying erratically. Was there something wrong with the vehicle or was he trying to avoid gunfire?

Nausea rose in her stomach. "Can you not do that with the copter?"

"If I don't do that, we'll be hit," he said.

That absolutely didn't make her feel better. Watching him guide them away from the island was watching a master at work. Instead of focusing on the unsteadiness of the chopper, she stared at Griffin's face. Intensity and concentration etched lines into his forehead. He was a handsome man, and her love for him swelled in her heart. She was certain of her feelings, but uncertain how to make him believe them.

After a time, the battle noises from the island faded. They were far enough away that explosions no longer rocked the air around them.

Griffin let out a curse.

"Is someone following us?" she asked.

"We're out of fuel. I'll bring it low, and we need to jump."

Jump into the water when it was dark? They wouldn't know what lurked in the ocean around them. "You want us to dive into the water? There are sharks. And eels."

"Don't think about that. Go into the back and look for a life raft and life jackets."

With fear making her dizzy, she searched. Metal compartments were latched closed. She checked inside each one. She found the life raft and in the cabinet below, three life vests. "I found them."

Had the boat been tested? What if it had a leak? How long had it been sitting in the helicopter, mildewing and rotting in the humidity? The idea of dangling in the water with her life vest on was terrifying. Not that the flimsy boat would provide much protection from aggressive, hungry sea life.

"Send a message to Kate West on the satellite phone that we've evacuated the base. She'll track the signal and send someone to pick us up," Griffin said.

Kit's hands were shaking so hard, it was difficult to type her SOS message. She read it three times to confirm she had the right information. "How are you calm right now?"

"Panicking doesn't improve the situation," he said.

She took a deep breath. "I sent the message." Her phone beeped. Kate had responded, acknowledging her message. They were tracking her location via the phone and redirecting the search and rescue team that had been deployed to the military base. How far away was the closest West Company team? "Help is on the way. No ETA."

The helicopter shuddered, and Kit grabbed a bar to steady herself.

"I need to lower the chopper into the water."

"Will it sink?" Being trapped inside a sinking vessel terrified her. "Should we just jump?" Their phone was cutting edge technology and waterproof and would keep them connected to the West Company.

"We have to stay together and I can't leave the copter without a pilot. It could crash anywhere, and kill someone," Griffin said.

Kit mustered her courage. "Tell me step-by-step what to do."

"Put on your life preserver. We'll jump, holding on to each other, and then inflate our boat. I'll help you into it first."

They put on their life vests. Griffin lowered the chopper. "If this comes out of my paycheck, I'm screwed," he said.

"I'll pay them back," Kit said.

"You have half a million dollars sitting around?" he asked.

"I have the money I was paid for giving up everything to focus on the Locker. I wasn't allowed to spend the money in a way that drew attention, so yes, I have most of it."

He let out a low whistle. "Okay, then. Distracted you long enough. Let's move. Ready to jump? Jump away from the chopper. We'll swim for a bit so we don't get pulled under."

If they split up in the water, it could be impossible to locate each other with the waves forcing them apart and the dark surrounding them.

Griffin held her hand and the boat, the water looking like black glass beneath them.

They jumped.

Chapter 13

The impact of hitting the water was shocking, and Griffin held on to Kit. She was tense, but at least she didn't squirm, because he was also gripping the lifeboat.

Maneuvering in the water and kicking away from the chopper, he opened the raft and pulled the tab to inflate it. Getting dry would pose a problem, and the wet and the cold would make it a necessity. He couldn't build a fire without risking their lives.

The helicopter was built to withstand limited contact with the water. Even as they waited to climb into the raft, the chopper tilted and began to sink under the water.

At least they were in the warm waters of a tropical region and not near the poles. Griffin had been in those waters before, and he'd had minutes to get dry and warm before hypothermia would have set in.

The raft inflated. Griffin helped Kit into it, then climbed inside. Kit was shivering. He didn't have dry clothes or a blanket. The contents of his backpack were soaked.

He gathered her against him, hoping to shield her from the wind and the air. When the sun rose, their clothes would dry out, but then they'd battle dehydration.

Wrapping their bodies together, Griffin held her. He had an odd sense of warmth and comfort that had nothing to do with how his body was feeling. Kit safe in his arms was what he needed most now.

"How are you feeling?" he asked.

"Cold. Tired. Do you see any boats?" she asked. She had tucked the phone into her life vest, and she removed it to look at it. "I can't turn this off. The West Company is using it to track us. But I don't have much battery left."

"We'll be okay. They'll find us."

He closed his eyes and centered himself. He knew the dangers on the open water. Rough waves could capsize them, the raft could leak and sink, sharks could confuse their raft for a tasty treat or unfriendly boats could find them.

In the distance, lightning flashed.

And a storm could be approaching, bringing torrential rains, rough waters and hazardous lightning.

Griffin hid his fear from Kit. If a storm was moving in their direction, they would need to stay calm and pray their luck held.

"Can you swim?" Griffin asked.

Kit's eyes grew wide. "Yes. A little."

He pulled the straps on her life vest to ensure they were tight. "We will get through this. Do you believe me?"

She swallowed hard and nodded. "You're worried about the storm."

He didn't want to upset her. "I've seen worse."

She buried her head into his neck. "I haven't."

The storm grew closer, the size of the waves increased and thunder rumbled. Water splashed into their boat. Griffin bailed it out. Kit watched him, quietly assessing the situation.

"We should have stayed on the island," Kit said, fright heavy in her voice.

They couldn't return to the island. They had to move forward with this plan. Incognito waited for them, and the United States military was likely furious at their actions. They had no allies in the vicinity, and zero at the military base. "We had to get away from Incognito. They were taking over the island, and they would have captured you. I couldn't let that happen."

The rain began to fall, soft and slow, but with every passing minute, harder and faster.

"Tell me the chances of surviving this," Kit said.

"High." Low. Very low. But telling her that wouldn't help. This was a challenge to stay calm and take each minute for what it was. "It's a passing shower." The storm clouds loomed overhead, gathering and rolling, protesting his words.

A bright light skimmed across the water from behind them. Griffin turned. A boat was moving in their direction. A rescue boat from the West Company? Incognito tracking them?

Griffin couldn't identify the boat by the shape.

He hated that Kit was in danger. Griffin had a weapon, but it was wet, and it might be useless against whatever threats waited on the approaching boat.

The boat stopped near them and threw them a rope. Griffin was reluctant to take it, but where else could they go? No motor, no paddles, no way to defend themselves against a storm and an unknown craft. They had to face whoever was on that boat. He grabbed the rope, and they were pulled toward the speedy watercraft.

Griffin helped Kit climb onto the boat, and he boarded after her. He and Kit were wet, cold and tired. The men on board pointed guns at them.

"Drop your backpack, phones and weapons on the deck," a man with a strange accent directed them.

Griffin's heart fell. He did as the man asked.

Griffin wasn't sure how to play this. Kit was pressed close to him, shaking. From the cold or from fear? Could these men be boaters on the water and being careful to protect themselves? Were they pirates? He and Kit had little of value to steal. Or had Incognito located them?

"Thanks for picking us up. Our boat sank," Griffin said. He could play it off like they were vacationers in the area.

"You've made things difficult for us," the man said. "We've been searching the globe for Kit Walker. Then your military gives away where she is." The man shifted, and Griffin noticed the Incognito spear tattoo on his neck.

They had a leak from someone on the island. Wonderful. Griffin would communicate that to Connor to be dealt with later.

"We don't want trouble," Griffin said.

"It doesn't matter what you want," the man said. "There's a high price on your heads, and I'm bringing you in to collect my reward."

After their escape, after everything they had done to evade Incognito, Kit had been captured.

Kit and Griffin were forced at gunpoint below-decks into a small, damp room. It was being used as a storage closet. Their hands were tied, they had been frisked and everything but their clothes had been taken. Had the boaters left the phone powered on, or had they destroyed it and tossed it into the water? Was the West Company tracking their signal? Would they realize something bad had happened and send additional search teams? A rescue team had been en route, but this situation was more complicated than the one they had described to Connor. Would the team he sent be prepared?

The West Company had the best, most highly trained operatives. Griffin had to believe whoever came for them would expect a fight.

They were alone in the small room. Griffin wouldn't stew on the sense of utter failure. "I'm sorry, Kit."

"For what?"

"For running us right into this trap," he said.

She moved closer and rubbed her shoulder against his. "I don't blame you for this. We would be in worse trouble if we had stayed on the island."

"We can't know what would have happened. Maybe the West Company would have found us in time."

"We'll get out of this," Kit said. "We've kept ourselves alive this far." She studied his face and cleared her throat. "I've thought of asking you this before, but you've been cagey about it. Why does it bother you so much to be in charge of protecting me? You're good at it. You've saved my life multiple times."

Could he tell her the truth? What would she think of him if he did? "I've kept you safe. But I haven't kept everyone safe."

"Another client?"

Somehow he had successfully completed missions involving clients. "My wife. My late wife."

Kit inhaled sharply. "You've never mentioned her."

Kit watched him intently, and he wanted to end the conversation. But she seemed anxious to know more, and he knew she would dig around about it. "I was overseas on a mission. I was scheduled to fly home, but I missed my flight. It was two a.m. her time, and I didn't want to call and wake her. While I waited for the next flight, I received a call from Connor that there had been a break-in at my house. My wife had come down the stairs, thinking an intruder was me, and had been killed by him." It had been the most devastating phone call of Griffin's life. Would Beth be alive if she had stayed in her bed? If she had stayed asleep? The robber, who was a repeat offender now serving a life sentence in prison, hadn't killed before. He had claimed that he hadn't planned to hurt anyone. He had thought no one was home.

"Griffin, I'm so sorry. That's terrible. You can't blame yourself for someone else's actions."

"I was due home, Kit. I was supposed to be on my way. I could have been home. If I was home, do you think I would have let my wife be killed?"

Kit laid her head on his shoulder. "I know that you would never let a client or someone you care about be hurt. I've seen you defend me again and again, at a cost to you. Your face is bruised. Your arms are covered in scratches. That was to protect me. You—"

The door opened to the small room, and Kit clamped her mouth shut.

A man with a doughy face, narrow eyes and an unlit cigarette hanging from his lips entered. "We're lucky we found you first. Word went out that you fled the island. There have to be a dozen boats and aircraft searching the Pacific for you."

Griffin's palms itched. He wouldn't let anyone hurt Kit. The boat had at least eight armed and trained men on board. They hadn't killed him and Kit outright. They'd want Kit alive to help them with the Locker.

Kit was quiet.

"You have no reason to fear us," said the man holding a gun across his chest.

Incognito had killed members of the Locker engineering team and had been partly responsible for Zoya's death. This group of sailors might be involved for the money and willing to kidnap for a big payday, but whom were he and Kit being delivered to?

The boat was speeding along, bouncing on the water. Any opening and Griffin would get Kit and himself out of this.

"We saved your life. You would have drowned," the man said again. The cigarette flopped up and down as he spoke. Was he trying to convince them he was a good person?

Kit and Griffin remained silent. Antagonizing the sailors wouldn't help, and Griffin had nothing to say on the matter.

The man ran his index finger down Kit's cheek. She twisted her head away. "Plenty of time to talk in the future."

Griffin didn't like anyone touching her without her permission. His hands were little use secured behind his back, but his legs could do damage. He struck out, knocking the man to the ground. Two others from the hallway moved in to subdue him. Griffin disabled them, as well.

"Untie my hands," he said to Kit. Before more kidnappers came to investigate, he needed his hands freed.

They turned back to back, and she untied his hands. When his were free, he did the same for her.

"What are we going to do?" she asked. She clung to him, and it wasn't the first time the weight of her safety fell squarely on his shoulders.

He held her in the band of his arms and wished he had a plan.

"Stay in this room with the door locked," Griffin said. "I will get control of the boat, and we'll figure out what to do after that." He kissed the top of her head, and she lifted her face to his.

Sliding his hand around the back of her neck, he kissed her fast on the mouth. He didn't offer an explanation. Her lips had been there for the taking, and he grabbed chances when he could. How many more opportunities would he have to kiss her and hold her? Every moment with her was precious. He should have enjoyed them more when they had been together instead of worrying about professionalism and the future.

Griffin turned to leave, and Kit grabbed his arm. "We should both get on deck and jump."

The boat pitched as if in warning about following such a risky plan. Griffin caught Kit before she slammed into the door. "Not in this storm."

"Do you know how to drive a boat?" she asked.

"Yes." More or less. He understood the gist of it. Don't hit anything and don't run it aground. "Stay here. Wait for me to get you." He would have felt better if Kit was with him, but if bullets started flying, he didn't want her caught in the crossfire.

"I believe in you. I know you can do this," Kit said. Those words on the tail end of his confession about his wife meant a lot to him. "If you can, find me a phone, a computer, anything. I'll send an SOS message to the West Company."

"Will do." Griffin slipped out of the room and waited to hear the door lock.

With the storm, the crew was focused on steering the boat and keeping it moving through the water. The boat was small enough that it was tossed by the waves. Griffin braced his legs as he walked. His limited experience on the water told him the boat was heaving too far left and right. They could capsize. Was it dangerous to leave Kit in the room?

Three men were seated in a small cabin near the ladder leading to the upper deck. A quick glance into the room told him nothing about their status. Were they armed?

The boat pitched again, and Griffin took advantage of the men being off-kilter to attack.

The first two men scrambled at him, fists swinging. Griffin had twenty pounds on them and years more fighting experience.

"Get out of the way. I'll shoot him," the third said.

A knockout punch to one attacker and a kick to the other and both were on the ground motionless. The third was holding a gun, aiming it at Griffin.

Griffin dove for his waist, ripping the gun from his hand and using it to strike him, rendering him unconscious. He left the men in the room.

Moving stealthily, Griffin climbed the ladder to the main deck. Two men were in the captain's perch, attempting to navigate the storm.

He stalked toward them, silence difficult with the boat rocking. One of the men must have sensed his approach. He turned, weapon in hand. He leveled his gun at Griffin and shot him, no warning given.

The bullet hit Griffin in the shoulder. The heat of the bullet lasted a moment before pain set in. Blood ran down his arm, dripping onto the gun he had stolen. He reached for the weapon with his other hand, preparing to defend himself.

The shooter aimed again. "Try it and I'll kill you."

"Stop, you fool. They're wanted alive," the other man said.

The shooter lowered his gun. "He came at me."

"Put him back in the storage room. Check the others. We'll hit land in twenty minutes."

Griffin's gun was taken and he was escorted back to the storage room. "Just because there's a better price on your head alive than dead doesn't mean I won't kill you if you make trouble. She's worth more, anyway."

Banging on the door yielded no response from Kit. Cursing, the shooter used his key to unlock it.

Griffin was pushed into the room and the door slammed shut behind him.

"Griffin!" Kit knelt next to him on the floor.

The room was spinning, the dip and sway of the boat not helping.

"What happened?" Kit asked, her hands scouring his body. At least he could still feel something.

"Shot in the shoulder."

Kit gasped as she looked at the wound. She ran to

a box in the room and opened it. "I saw some blankets in here. We'll use them to stop the bleeding."

She pressed a blanket over his shoulder, and he gritted his teeth. He wouldn't scream in front of her. It wasn't the most pain he'd been in, but unconsciousness pulled at the edges of his vision. He had to stay alert. He wasn't much good to Kit in any case, but he couldn't leave her alone.

Kit went to the door and tried to open it. It was locked. She pounded her fist against it. "Someone better bring me a first aid kit and bandages. Do you hear me? We need medical help! He'll bleed to death!"

Griffin closed his eyes, focusing on staying conscious. How long would mind over matter work?

Kit returned to him, pressing on his shoulder. He opened his eyes. Tears were running down her face.

"Hey, stop. No crying. We'll be fine," he said. Was he slurring his words? They sounded garbled to him.

Kit pressed on his shoulder and lay next to him. "Tell me what to do. Just tell me what I can do to fix this."

The boat bumped against something hard and then drew to a stop. Kit sat up, her eyes wide with fear. "Did we hit something?"

The door to the cabin flew open. The man who had been driving the boat pointed to them. "Get up. We have an appointment."

Kit wiped at the water on her face, wanting to appear strong. Her tears and sweat were mixing with the rain. Griffin was walking next to her, and she didn't know how he was managing. He had lost a lot of blood from his shoulder. His cheek was swollen and his lip was cut, injuries sustained on the island. He needed a hospital immediately.

Anger swelled inside her. Anger at Incognito, thinking they could use people in whatever manner they wanted to pursue their cause. Anger at the West Company, which was supposed to protect them. Anger at herself for not being more careful, for not taking the money she had earned working on the Locker and disappearing. She had wanted to be near her family, but once she had made the decision to work on a top secret, dangerous government mission, she had given up her freedom.

At the end of the dock, a man waited for them. He was dressed in black and in need of a shave.

"Welcome to our island," he said. "I am Cypher."

Their island? "My… Griffin needs medical attention," she said.

Cypher looked at Griffin. "Whether or not he receives it depends on you."

"What do you want from me?" Kit asked.

"You're a smart woman. You must have figured that out by now."

Dread curled in her stomach. "The Locker. You want me to do something with the Locker."

"I knew you were smart. Don't disappoint me."

"Griffin needs medical attention now. Fix him first. Then I'll help you."

"You are not in a position to make demands," Cypher said.

"You are not in a position to test me. You need me. Otherwise you wouldn't have bothered putting a price on my head," Kit said.

Cypher rubbed his bearded chin and then sighed. He took his phone from his pocket and spoke into it. "I need a medic at the pier."

As the rain pelted them, Griffin slipped to his knees. Kit wrapped her arms around him. She would protect him as he had protected her too many times.

A red pickup truck pulled up to the pier, and a woman in a purple rain jacket carrying a tote bag climbed out. She looked at Griffin and then at Kit. "Help me get him into my truck. I can't see enough to work out here."

Kit helped carry Griffin to the pickup and climbed into the back with him.

"You stay with us," Cypher said.

Kit shook her head. They could take Griffin anywhere and kill him. She was staying at his side. "I'll see that he is cared for first. Then I will help you."

Cypher nodded. The medic climbed in the car and drove the short distance to a warehouse. The warehouse was less beaten than the other buildings in the vicinity, with fewer smashed windows. Was this an Incognito base of operations located close to a United States military base and yet undetected?

"Griffin, can you hear me? Everything will be okay. They have someone to take care of you," Kit said.

His chest was rising and falling, but his eyes were closed. "I was supposed to take care of you," he said.

"You have taken care of me," she said.

"Not well enough," he said.

Not this again. Kit took his face in her hands. "Stop that. Needing help from time to time isn't a weakness. I'm sorry that you think what happened with your late wife will happen to every other person in your life, but it won't. You tell me to think positive. Nothing bad will happen to me, not as long as we are together." She stroked his hair.

"Love you, Kit," he said.

Did he say he loved her? "Griffin?"

He didn't respond. The medic parked the car. She and Kit, with the help of a couple of Incognito terrorists, carried Griffin's dead weight into the warehouse and into a small room with an examination table in the middle and medical equipment.

The medic cut Griffin's clothing away from his shoulder. She inspected the wound. "Good thing he passed out. I'm low on morphine, and this will hurt. I have to dig the bullet out of his shoulder."

Kit took Griffin's hand. The medic worked on his shoulder. Griffin's body was covered in sweat, and he periodically shivered.

Kit prayed for Griffin and she prayed for their safe rescue. It seemed like hours had passed. Kit watched Griffin's stomach, his breathing her only comfort.

Finally the medic pulled off her gloves. "I've done all I can. Bullet is out and I've stitched and bandaged it, but he needs a hospital. Whatever you're asked to do, you better do it fast."

"What is this place?" Kit asked.

"I can't say. I'm sorry," the medic said. She spoke not another word and fled the room, leaving Kit alone with Griffin.

His breathing seemed even. Kit had no medical training. She didn't know what signs indicated he was healing. Incognito cared about Griffin's health only in that keeping him alive forced Kit to help them. Kit set her hand over his heart, reassuring herself Griffin was breathing.

The door opened again. This time two armed guards appeared with a battered-looking man between them. The prisoner lifted his head, and shock rolled through her.

"Arsenic," Kit said.

When Arsenic saw Kit, he narrowed his eyes as if trying to focus. "What are you doing here?" Arsenic asked.

"We were brought here," Kit said.

"They will kill us no matter what we do," Arsenic said. "They have Stargazer." His voice was devoid of emotion.

Kit's eyes grew wide. "How? He's…sick."

"He is sick. He has been for a long time," Arsenic said. "Incognito has been questioning him. Stargazer can't do anything. He can't answer them. Their patience is wearing thin. If we can't make the Locker work, they'll kill us. All of us."

A chill of terror shot down her spine. Incognito had gathered her, Arsenic and Stargazer in the same location. If they wanted to steal or reengineer the

Locker for their purposes, they had the dream team, at least on paper.

The guards pushed Arsenic into the room and then closed the door behind him. Kit heard the door lock. What mind game was this, and could Kit outsmart them?

Griffin heard voices and waited until he and Kit were alone with Arsenic. Griffin pushed himself to sitting and took in the room. "We're leaving this island." His shoulder was throbbing, and he felt nauseated and weak.

"How?" Arsenic asked. He seemed weary and ragged.

"We'll find a way," Kit said.

Arsenic's right leg was wrapped with bandages that had turned dark red.

"What happened to your leg?" Kit asked.

"Do you think they brought me here willingly?" he asked.

"Can you walk?" Griffin asked. Whatever had happened, he would have medical attention when they were off the island.

"I can walk," the older man said.

Arsenic was in pain, but he seemed clear-headed. Formulating a plan, Griffin pointed between Kit and Arsenic. "Kit, help him, and I'll clear a path."

"What about Stargazer?" Kit asked.

"Do you know where he is?" Griffin asked Arsenic.

"I've heard him screaming. He must be close. Maybe inside the warehouse," Arsenic said.

What state would he be in? If Stargazer had lost his mind during the building of the Locker and was now being held against his will and tortured by Incognito, he might be in no shape to flee. He might fight them and refuse to leave. Was it worth the risk to look for him? Griffin could send reinforcements when they were safe.

A man with wild brown hair stepped into the room. His T-shirt hung limply on his thin frame, and his jeans were old and worn. "Thank you for making this easy for me."

"Stargazer!" Kit said.

Griffin was surprised that he was safe and alive. Stargazer's mental state was another matter, of course. What was Stargazer dealing with? Paranoia? Delusions?

Kit started to run to him with her arms open, but Griffin stopped her. Something about this wasn't right. They were keeping Stargazer locked up, and now he was waltzing into this makeshift medical room to speak with them?

Stargazer smiled and leveled a gun at them. "I'm in charge now. What I say goes."

Stargazer stared at Kit. "Whatever you did to the Locker, undo it. We'll have a brainstorming session. We'll get the Locker running. This time, under my terms. Defy me, and your boyfriend dies. Looks like he's half-dead anyway."

Kit moved in front of Griffin. "Leave him alone."

"He's made my plans much more difficult," Stargazer said.

"You were in the hospital," Kit said. "You were sick. How did you get here?"

"You were being tortured," Arsenic said, sounding as shocked as Kit was.

Stargazer let out a bark of laughter. "I got the idea from you, Arsenic. You faked a stroke. I pretended to be crazy. Only good old hardworking, naive Kit stuck with the project. If she had snapped and quit, the Locker would be one more failed government project."

Griffin moved to get a better vantage on Stargazer and put himself between the gun and Kit.

"I am touched to know that you were worried about me," Stargazer said and put his hand over his chest. "Trying to protect me. I knew that was how you'd respond if you thought I was in trouble."

"Why do you work for Incognito?" Kit asked.

Stargazer snorted. "I don't. You're sadly out of the loop. Haven't you figured it out yet?"

Stargazer was dangerous. He had a large spear tattoo the length of his forearm. That was all the information Griffin needed. Stargazer was enemy number one at the moment, deeply involved with Incognito.

"The Locker is worth nothing. But the information it is protecting is worth billions. I realized I could be the auctioneer in an amazing public sale of classified information to interested groups. There are many parties who were willing to partner with me and provide the manpower I needed to make it happen. Break into the Locker, get access to every high-value piece of data and then sell it," Stargazer said.

Top secret documents, classified identities and government secrets were in high demand. Warfare wasn't about guns and bombs. It was maneuvering and mind games and double agents.

"You're the mastermind behind the Locker. You could hack into it yourself," Kit said. "You don't need us."

Stargazer pinned her with a look. "I invented it. I built some of it. I thought when Arsenic left and I faked a breakdown, you would have lost your mind. You were so young and fragile and expected perfection. No one can survive under those circumstances. But you surprised me. You stuck with it, and I couldn't break your work. That might make you a genius, but it also makes you a pain in my ass."

Griffin heard helicopters overhead. Was it the West Company or members of Incognito returning from their assault on the United States military base? If they had ever needed a savior, now was the time.

Stargazer pointed his weapon at Griffin, and Kit's heart felt like it would explode. How much more could Griffin take? He had to be in extreme pain.

"If only you had left Kit at the safe house on day one, we could have avoided all this. No unnecessary injuries and deaths," Stargazer said.

"Stop it!" Kit shouted. "If you want me to fix what I did on the island, give me a computer and leave Griffin alone."

Stargazer leveled a look at her. "Don't call for help. You need the connection to the Locker, perhaps, but don't attempt to send a request for help."

Her face must have been defiant and angry. Kit pictured herself flying at Stargazer, fists swinging and knocking his smug, skinny self on his butt. "I will give you what you want. I can get you access to the files." She wasn't sure she could, but with Stargazer holding a gun on them, she would have promised him anything. Buy them some time. She would find a way out of this. She met Griffin's eyes. "I will get you home."

The corners of Griffin's mouth turned up, not quite into a smile. "I'm supposed to save you."

"You've saved me plenty. It's my turn." She wouldn't tell him she loved him again. If Stargazer knew how much Griffin meant to her, he'd use Griffin to manipulate her even more.

Giving access to the documents breached laws and ethics and her personal moral code. But if she couldn't stall under these circumstances, what choice did she have?

Stargazer pressed a button on the wall, and a cabinet opened. A laptop slid out. "Use that one. Get the job done."

Kit waited for the computer to boot up. "Griffin needs a hospital. He needs meds and proper treatment."

"Our medic looked at him," Stargazer said.

Griffin was sweating and he was pale. He was trying to hide his pain but couldn't from her. She knew him too well. "That's not enough."

Stargazer sneered. "Then it looks like you're on a tight timeline. Work now. I'm watching you."

Kit began typing.

Help would come. Someone would save Griffin.

From his place leaning against the wall, Griffin collected himself. He'd been hurt worse, and while he needed a doctor to look at his shoulder, he was fine for now. It would take longer for infection to set in. He was playing up his injury, letting Stargazer underestimate him. It was the best time to strike.

Stargazer's gun dipped. He was narrowing his eyes, watching the computer screen as Kit typed. When Stargazer's shoulders relaxed, Griffin launched himself at the Incognito leader, catching the man unaware. Griffin used his weight to drag him to the ground. Stargazer hit Griffin's shoulder, which twisted his pain into anger.

Griffin tore the gun from Stargazer's hand. "Call for backup and I'll shoot before anyone has time to react. I'll make this bullet count. No medic will be able to save you." For good measure, he punched Stargazer across the face, rendering the man unconscious.

The fire alarm blared, and a strobe light on the wall blinked.

"I set off the alarms that the island was under attack and everyone should abandon their posts," Kit said from the terminal. "We need to go."

She had created a perfect distraction.

Griffin hauled himself to his feet. "We'd better get off this island now."

Finding the energy to run wasn't easy. He was lightheaded, and staying conscious took effort.

Kit stood at his side and Arsenic moved to the other. Together they fled the warehouse. As they ran, alarms sounded, but the trio was ignored. Men poured toward the docks. It would be harder to blend or steal a boat with so many Incognito agents rushing to flee.

"We need another way off the island," Griffin said.

Kit grinned. "That was part two of my escape plan. The West Company knows right where we are. Help is on the way."

Griffin, Arsenic and Kit hid behind a row of parked cars. When the unmarked fleet of choppers set down near the pier, Griffin knew the West Company had arrived.

Kit wrapped her arms around Griffin's waist. "Griffin, I need you to know that I love you. This is over, but I love you."

Griffin held a hand to his ear. "What? I can't hear you."

Was he pretending he couldn't hear to avoid this discussion? "I love you."

Those three words were clear.

Griffin stroked the side of her face. "We need to talk."

She couldn't read Griffin's expression. Arsenic was watching the exchange, but when Kit glanced in his direction, he looked away.

"When?" Kit asked. If these helicopters whisked Griffin to another mission with a new identity, how would she find him again?

Chapter 14

The West Company headquarters in Wisconsin was a nondescript building near the Ottawa National Forest. The sign on the building announced it was a nature conservancy.

After Griffin's and Arsenic's injuries had been treated, she, Griffin and Arsenic had been brought to Wisconsin for questioning. Kit felt foggy and scared as she sat in the conference room with Connor West and Griffin.

"You sent worldwide, critical systems into lockdown mode," Connor West said.

Kit wouldn't deny it. "Yes. I had to. To protect the data. Incognito was too close."

"It wasn't your call to make," Connor said.

They had no way to spin blame away from her.

CIA, NSA and military leaders were pissed. Their record systems were still in lockdown, and they wanted answers.

"I did what I thought was best," Kit said.

Connor slanted her a look. "We've interrogated the Incognito agents we've captured from the island. They've been making plea deals and providing information about Incognito in exchange for lighter prison sentences."

"What about Stargazer?" Kit asked.

"He's in federal custody. Unlikely he will be able to negotiate a lesser punishment," Connor said. "We're close to destroying the copies of the code they stole and tracking Incognito groups around the globe."

"That's great news," Kit said. She and Griffin were in trouble, but from the moment they had been rescued from the island, they had been separated. He was seated in the room with her, but he had not looked at her or spoken a single word. Her heart ached. She wished he would say something to her.

"The West Company is assembling a team to bring the government's systems back online safely," Connor said.

This was supposed to be a debriefing, but Kit felt like she was being put under a microscope. She was in trouble, certainly, but what about Griffin? Would he be okay?

After a tap on the door, Kate West entered the room. She was hugely pregnant, wearing a stylish printed maxidress and cardigan. Her husband's face lit up when he saw her. For a man who otherwise showed no emotion, it was touching to witness.

Connor kissed Kate's cheek and then touched her belly protectively. "Are you sure you're up for this?"

Kate set her hand over her husband's and smiled at him. "I know when to take a break. The opportunity to work with Kit will be a pleasure."

Kit felt a twinge of jealousy for the well-known computer scientist who had found love and romance and was having a baby with her rich, handsome and devoted husband.

Some women were dealt the best cards. Others were dealt no cards in the love and romance department.

"I haven't asked her if she wants to be part of the team," Connor said.

Kate sat and smiled at Kit. "Knowing you did your best with what you had at the time, the United States government is willing to overlook the incident with the Locker that occurred on the island if you're willing to be part of the team building and securing the systems we need to protect."

Kit hadn't expected this. "What about the Locker?"

"That project is being decommissioned. It's too risky to allow one security blanket to cover us. We have other plans in place," Kate said.

Intriguing work. "Sounds like a long-term commitment," Kit said, glancing at Griffin, wondering what he was thinking.

"It is. A job for as long as you'd like it," Kate said.

"I don't want to live in isolation again," Kit said.

Kate nodded. "You would be working from this building. You are free to live your life on your time. No strings."

"Would I be working with Griffin?" Kit asked. She looked at him.

A muscle in Griffin's jaw flexed. He was upset but keeping his mouth shut. What was on his mind?

Kate glanced between the two of them. "Oh. I can't believe I missed this."

Not an answer. Kit waited for someone to respond.

Kate stood. "We could make arrangements for you two to work together periodically. But why don't we leave you to discuss that?"

Connor gave his wife a bewildered look. "I need to debrief Griffin."

Kate squeezed her husband's arm. "Give them a minute. They need to talk."

Connor looked from his wife to Griffin and Kit. Realization about their personal relationship must have dawned. "It's been a rough few days. We'll be back in a few minutes."

Connor and Kate left the room, closing the door behind them.

Kit had so much to say, she didn't know where to start. "Griffin, I want this job."

Griffin folded his hands on the table. "Then take it."

He was not factoring their relationship into her acceptance of the job. "You won't mind seeing me?" she asked.

"I travel. It's not a big deal. I'm rarely at headquarters, usually only between assignments. That is, if I still have a job and am not put in prison."

"I already told them I disabled the Locker. You won't be in trouble for this," Kit said. "But do you want to see me?" The question came out squeaky, and Kit wished she had spoken more strongly.

"I told you from the start that my commitment is to my job. When I'm off medical leave, I'll go where I'm needed."

Then he wanted this to be the end of their personal relationship. After everything they had been through, he was finished with her. "I see."

He looked at her, and his green eyes pierced her. "Kit, don't be upset. You've known from the beginning that our relationship had a shelf life."

She felt tears pressing at her eyes. He had been honest with her, but she wasn't ready to accept that this was over. "Then this is goodbye?"

Griffin stood. He crossed the room to her and with his good arm, he hugged her. "It has to be. I don't see another way."

Kate had said they could work together, but Griffin was ignoring that. He didn't want them to work together. He wanted to be free of her.

Now, if only her heart could be free of him.

Griffin held his hand up to Kit's door three times before he knocked. He could have left the States, and whatever words were spoken between them would have needed to be enough. Something about the look in her eyes haunted him. Flying to the other side of the world and being unable to contact her would mean the last time they'd spoken, he had upset her. He couldn't live with that.

Griffin held his mission orders in his hand. He had to say good-bye to Kit properly, explain what he could and wish her the best. He was wheels up in three hours, which left little time to pack and no time for discussions. He hated leaving Kit, but he was no longer her protector. Accepting that was hard.

Kit was working from the West Company's headquarters, the safest place in the Midwest. Nothing bad would happen to her. He had to believe that or he wouldn't be able to leave. After what had happened to Beth, he needed to know that Kit would not suffer the same fate.

Kit opened her door. Surprise registered on her face. She lowered the candy bar she was eating from her mouth. "Griffin. I thought you'd left."

Disappointed to see him? Angry he had come by? "I'm leaving soon."

She stared at him. A bit of chocolate beckoned to him from her lower lip. He wanted to kiss it from her mouth. "Can I come in?"

She stepped back from the door, allowing him inside. He set his heavy pack on the floor. The apartment was cozy and bright, like Kit. "This is your new place?" he asked.

"We don't have to make small talk. This is a lease from the West Company until I find a place of my own."

"It's nice."

She lifted her brow impatiently. "How long will you be gone?"

Until the job was done and Incognito couldn't hurt Kit. "A day. A week. Months." Her safety remained his top priority. The West Company was tasked with using the information they'd acquired to root out members of Incognito. Griffin had volunteered to be part of that team.

Kit remained silent. "What will I do?"

Was she asking if she should wait for him to return, to put their relationship in some type of paused state? He couldn't ask or expect her to do that. "You'll work for the West Company."

Kit fell back a couple of steps. The distance between them had never been greater.

"Arsenic agreed to work on the team," Kit said.

The sadness in her voice gutted him. She was speaking as if she was fine, but Griffin knew she wasn't. This mission has morphed from professional to something else entirely. Did she understand that he couldn't stay at her side while dangers lurked in the world, dangers that were targeting her? That he was leaving because he loved her and wanted to keep her safe?

Loved her. He loved her. The truth struck him so hard, it knocked the air from his lungs.

He wanted to give her a clean break from him. He owed her. Walking away wasn't easy. What he felt for her shouldn't have been her burden. "I wish you the best." Not the words he had been looking for. They expressed nothing of what he felt or the deep, burning desire to keep her safe. They didn't communicate that he wanted to make feverish love to her today and when he returned and every day after that.

He couldn't say those things to her. He wouldn't make promises he couldn't keep.

Her hand gripped her candy bar harder, and her free hand rolled into a fist. "Is that how you say goodbye to me?" The heat in her eyes did crazy things to his pulse.

He had another way he wanted to say goodbye. Would she let him touch her? He went for broke, lifting her in his arms. He kissed her hard on the mouth and tasted caramel and chocolate and almonds. Her candy bar hit the floor. He kicked the door closed and headed for the bedroom.

He'd had great sex before, but he couldn't define what he had with Kit as just great sex. When they were alone together, they existed on some other plane. It wasn't quickie sex or because-it-feels-good sex. This was altogether different. He cared about her. He wanted her to be happy. He wanted to be the man who made her happy.

He cradled her against him, loving the feel of her body pressed to his. She wrapped her arms around his neck. In one smooth motion, he laid her on the bed and lowered his body on top of hers.

He interlaced his right hand with her left and brought her fingers to his lips. He kissed each knuckle. An invisible force held him close to her. He hadn't come to her apartment to make love to her.

He'd wanted to explain something, but now words weren't enough.

Seeing her, holding her in his arms, he was lost. She reached for his shirt, and he let her undress him. When he was totally naked, he lay back on the bed. She ran her fingers through his hair, and then trailed her hand down his face, across his chest and stomach. He loved that she liked his body and could enjoy him.

He wanted to flip her onto her back and make slow love to her. She would set the pace. This was her music they were dancing to. He wouldn't push her even if he wanted her more than he had ever wanted another woman. Even though watching her was making him hot. His arousal was desperate for her touch.

"Why did you come here?" she asked.

He wouldn't lie even though the answer would hurt her. "To say good-bye." He couldn't stay away. He should have been on his way to the airport. He should have been checking his supplies, reading his trip documents. But he had been drawn to her. He'd needed to see her, to resolve those unspoken problems between them.

Sadness touched the corners of her eyes, and she pressed a kiss to his lips. Her intentions were plain. She removed her clothes, never breaking contact. Withdrawing a condom from his wallet, she rolled it on.

Razor-sharp desire piercing him, he called on his control. As slow as she wanted it, however she wanted him, tonight was for her.

She melted against him, and he kissed her with

the pent-up longing dwelling inside him. Shifting her hips, she impaled herself on him in one hard thrust. He groaned and reached to where their bodies were joined, finding the spot she liked him to touch.

She adjusted her legs and rode him, rocking her hips and letting her body guide her motions. Her breaths were shallow and he lifted his hips, pushing against her and trying to stay calm. He needed to make this last.

Everything she did, every sound from her lips, every brush of her fingertips threatened to push him over. He wouldn't last much longer. He turned her onto her back and worked his hips, delving inside her, losing himself completely. The sensations of her release triggered his own.

As his pulse began to slow, he extracted himself and cleaned up. She hadn't moved from the bed, but she was awake, watching him.

"I wish you were mine," she said.

The statement pierced his heart. He searched for the words to accomplish what he had come here to do. "My job is my life and right now, my job is to keep you safe, to find the members of Incognito. To stop them. To make sure you can live your life without looking over your shoulder. When I went overseas and Beth was killed, it was like a part of me had died, too."

Kit watched him, saying nothing, just listening.

"I couldn't forgive myself. My occupation means I should be able to keep the people I care for safe. I wasn't careful enough with Beth."

"The person responsible for Beth's death is Beth's attacker," Kit said.

"I know that here." He touched his head and then brought his hand to his heart. "But here, I feel if I can't keep you safe, then what good am I?"

She blinked at him and propped herself on her elbow. "Is that what this is about? You think in order to keep me safe you have to finish the mission against Incognito by rooting out every last terrorist involved with the organization?"

If Incognito knew Kit was alive and where she was, they would come after her. "It's the only way."

"The only way for what?" she asked. "To protect me? Because Griffin, I will be a target of other groups. I work for the West Company now. I won't advertise my occupation, but plenty of bad guys want to stop me and my work."

He stroked a strand of hair behind her ear, taking in her words.

"Am I safer with you globetrotting around the world, or am I safer with you at my side, protecting me, with us protecting each other? When we're together, we're amazing, and I feel safe. It's being apart too much that scares me."

He hadn't thought about it in those terms. "Together. How would it work? How could I do my work out in the world and you do yours in an office?"

She stroked the side of his face. "We could travel together. Take on missions together. When we need to be apart, it won't be for long. I told you once before I love you, and I'll love you enough for the both of us."

Griffin kissed her. He loved her. He knew it with every fiber of his being. "You won't have to do that. I love you, Kit."

Tears filled her eyes. "You love me?"

"Isn't it obvious?"

She threw herself into his arms and kissed him. "I needed the words."

"And now that you have them and me?"

"We'll work something out together. Together will always be our right answer."

* * * * *

Don't miss these other suspenseful stories
by C.J. Miller:

GUARDING HIS ROYAL BRIDE
THE SECRET KING
TRAITOROUS ATTRACTION
TAKEN BY THE CON

Available now from
Harlequin Romantic Suspense!

REQUEST YOUR FREE BOOKS!
2 FREE NOVELS PLUS 2 FREE GIFTS!

ROMANTIC suspense

Sparked by danger, fueled by passion

YES! Please send me 2 FREE Harlequin® Romantic Suspense novels and my 2 FREE gifts (gifts are worth about $10). After receiving them, if I don't wish to receive any more books, I can return the shipping statement marked "cancel." If I don't cancel, I will receive 4 brand-new novels every month and be billed just $4.74 per book in the U.S. or $5.49 per book in Canada. That's a savings of at least 12% off the cover price! It's quite a bargain! Shipping and handling is just 50¢ per book in the U.S. and 75¢ per book in Canada.* I understand that accepting the 2 free books and gifts places me under no obligation to buy anything. I can always return a shipment and cancel at any time. Even if I never buy another book, the two free books and gifts are mine to keep forever.

240/340 HDN GH3P

Name _____ (PLEASE PRINT) _____

Address _____ Apt. # _____

City _____ State/Prov. _____ Zip/Postal Code _____

Signature (if under 18, a parent or guardian must sign) _____

Mail to the **Reader Service:**
IN U.S.A.: P.O. Box 1867, Buffalo, NY 14240-1867
IN CANADA: P.O. Box 609, Fort Erie, Ontario L2A 5X3

**Want to try two free books from another line?
Call 1-800-873-8635 or visit www.ReaderService.com.**

* Terms and prices subject to change without notice. Prices do not include applicable taxes. Sales tax applicable in N.Y. Canadian residents will be charged applicable taxes. Offer not valid in Quebec. This offer is limited to one order per household. Not valid for current subscribers to Harlequin Romantic Suspense books. All orders subject to credit approval. Credit or debit balances in a customer's account(s) may be offset by any other outstanding balance owed by or to the customer. Please allow 4 to 6 weeks for delivery. Offer available while quantities last.

Your Privacy—The Reader Service is committed to protecting your privacy. Our Privacy Policy is available online at www.ReaderService.com or upon request from the Reader Service.

We make a portion of our mailing list available to reputable third parties that offer products we believe may interest you. If you prefer that we not exchange your name with third parties, or if you wish to clarify or modify your communication preferences, please visit us at www.ReaderService.com/consumerchoice or write to us at Reader Service Preference Service, P.O. Box 9062, Buffalo, NY 14240-9062. Include your complete name and address.

Tension wafted from Josie. "It's just like my father described—the tree, the carvings and the creek."

"Did he tell you what the carvings meant?"

She shook her head. "No, I'm not even sure he's the one who made them."

"Then, let's see if we can dig up an old watch," he replied.

They hadn't quite reached the front of the tree when a man stepped out from behind it, a gun in his hand.

Josie released a sharp yelp of surprise and Tanner tightened his grip on the shovel. What in the hell was going on? Did this man have something to do with whatever had happened to Eldridge?

"Josie Colton," he said, his thin lips twisting into a sneer. "I knew if I tailed you long enough you'd lead me to the watch. I've been watching you for days."

"Who are you?" Josie asked.

"That's for me to know and you not to find out," he replied. "Now, about that watch…"

"What watch?" she replied. "I—I don't know what you're talking about." Her voice held a tremor that belied her calm demeanor.

Tanner didn't move a muscle although his brain fired off in a dozen different directions. The man had called her by name, so this obviously had nothing to do with Eldridge.

Why would a man with a gun know about a watch wanted for sentimental reasons? What hadn't Josie told him? Was it possible to disarm the man without anyone getting hurt?

"Don't play dumb with me, girlie." The man raised a hand to sweep a hank of oily dark hair out of his eyes. "Your daddy spent years in prison bragging about how he was going to be buried with that cheap watch and then nobody would ever find the map to all the money from those old bank heists." He took a step toward them. "Now tell me where that watch is. I want that map."

Adrenaline pumped through Tanner. He certainly didn't know anything about old bank robberies, but a sick danger snapped in the air.

A look of deadly menace radiated outward from the gunman's dark, beady eyes. The gun was steady in his hands, and Tanner's chest constricted.

He tightened his grip on the shovel, calculated the distance between himself and the gunman's arm and then he swung. The end of the shovel connected. The gun fell from the man's grasp, but not before he fired off a shot.

The woods exploded with sound—the boom of the gun, a flutter of birds' wings overhead as they flew out of the treetops and Josie's scream of unmistakable pain.

Don't miss
COLTON COWBOY HIDEOUT by New York Times
bestselling author Carla Cassidy,
available July 2016 wherever
Harlequin® Romantic Suspense
books and ebooks are sold.

www.Harlequin.com

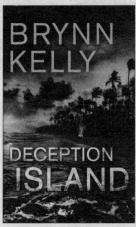

Turn your love of reading into
rewards you'll love with

Harlequin My Rewards

**Join for FREE today at
www.HarlequinMyRewards.com**

Earn **FREE BOOKS** of your choice.

Experience **EXCLUSIVE OFFERS** and contests.

Enjoy **BOOK RECOMMENDATIONS**
selected just for you.

PLUS! Sign up now
and get **500** points
right away!

Earn
FREE
REWARDS
Join
Today!
HarlequinMyRewards.com

MYR16R

JUST CAN'T GET ENOUGH?

Join our social communities
and talk to us online.

You will have access to the latest
news on upcoming titles and special
promotions, but most importantly,
you can talk to other fans about your
favorite Harlequin reads.

Harlequin.com/Community

Facebook.com/HarlequinBooks

Twitter.com/HarlequinBooks

Pinterest.com/HarlequinBooks